Love and the LAWLESS

volume one
a love africa press collection

First Published in Great Britain in 2019 by
LOVE AFRICA PRESS
103 Reaver House, 12 East Street, Epsom KT17 1HX
www.loveafricapress.com

ISBN: 978-1-9161546-4-3
Also available as eBook

Introducing the antiheroes of the Love Africa Press collections:

Dauntless and indomitable, brutal and lethal, these dark heroes take no prisoners in their quests for retribution. And when love shines a light into their lives, they will protect their beloveds no matter the costs.

PURPLE AND WHITE by Emem Bassey

Rono is a vigilante mafia prince with a dangerous plan to avenge his father's death.
Suto is a genius medical doctor not afraid to get her hands dirty to pay off her father's debt.
A marriage of convenience between these two could solve their problems. But what happens when love complicates matters and betrayal rears its ugly head?

CHAPTER ONE

Outskirt of Uyo

"Yes! Yes, I did it!" the man sobbed, his head dropping over his chest as he heaved, blood dripping from his mouth and soaking his lilac shirt.

Rono Ating stood ramrod straight and wondered why Oscar had decided to confess after his face had been beaten to an unrecognizable pulp. He could have done it when he'd not been touched at all.

"The prize was enticing, and Jacob ... your father, never thought me worthy enough to sit in his dealings." Oscar sneered; it could be heard in the tone of his voice, because his battered face proved unable to portray that emotion.

"So, you thought it would be a good idea to betray him." Rono chuckled, looking round the decrepit warehouse. "Who?"

Oscar knew not to pretend he didn't understand the question. He listed out names of people, business partners Rono's father had regarded as close associates.

"And Felicia?" Rono looked at the tied up man, hoping to get more from the shift of his eyes, but he spat in disgust.

"I know nothing about your fuck bitch. There was talk about kidnapping her to put you in a fix, but someone said she wasn't worth anything to you."

"My father must have seen through your pretence ... and your recent group of friends do, too."

"What do you mean?"

"Thank you, Oscar, for the list, but it's quite unfortunate you won't be paying for my laundry," Rono commented while staring at his blood-stained white shirt, a result of beating on Oscar.

It took a while for Oscar to understand his meaning. Fear broke through the passiveness of his battered face when Rono pointed the gun at his head.

"Plea—"

His head exploded on the warehouse floor before he could complete the single syllable word.

Rono stood there staring at the mess while examining how he felt at just killing a man, ending his destiny, as it were. Was that a twinge at the darkest part of his heart? He mentally shook his head. No twinge, not when he recalled his father's unmoving body at the mortuary as clear as when he'd stared at it. His mind refused to forget the cloying scent of formalin and the cold. He'd not had to touch his father to feel the cold; it had wafted from his still body.

No twinge now—there had to be none, not when his vibrant father was six feet under and worm food. His aim was to send his betrayers to the worms, too.

"Where is his car?" he asked one of his goons.

"Parked around the corner, Boss."

Rono nodded. "Both of you, make this look like a robbery, and then call me to know where I am for the next clean up."

"Yes, Boss."

CHAPTER TWO

Uyo Metropolis

Rono was unworried about the route his driver was taking and seemingly more so about the fact that someone would die by the end of the night, for having the temerity to kidnap his so-called girlfriend and still remain in town.

Not that he loved her; far from it. When she'd not returned to his house eight nights prior, he'd been relieved that she'd finally gotten the memo and had left. He'd tried calling her, but her number had been switched off. He'd assumed she'd returned home, but then, her father had called him two nights ago asking to speak with his daughter as her phone wasn't going through.

"I thought she was with you?" he'd croaked, barely keeping his eyes open.

Rono had pulled his phone from his ear when Ekwere had gone ballistic over the disappearance of his daughter. The old man claimed Felicia had gone missing under Rono's watch, and that's what he'd be telling the police.

Rono shook his head. Added to hunting his dad's killers, he had to find that nuisance. Hopefully, she was alive, so he could disentangle from her once and for all. He was done with her pestilence.

If he confirmed his findings and had to kill Okoko, it would be purely on principle, as was expected in the underworld. Revenge was taken for any and all slights; case in point, the two men he'd killed so far in avenging his father's murder and the few more lined up.

"We're here," his driver informed.

"Thanks, Abel. Inform the guys in the backup car that I'll be doing this one alone until otherwise advised."

"Yes, Boss." The driver picked up his two-way phone as Rono opened the back door of the Range Rover Sport 2015 model.

He was tall enough to step down from the black, sleek SUV without awkwardly sliding down from the high seat. His sharp gaze scanned the estate as his hands arranged his teal blue suit over the sprinkle of blood stains on his white shirt.

Rono was grateful for the security man's absence; it saved him from answering dumb questions. He recalled coming here with his father, and they'd had to wait for the security guy to call Okoko before letting them in.

He pressed the doorbell knowing there would not be questions, seeing as he had passed the first layer of security; members of this household would assume he was a usual friend of the family.

They needed to change their security man.

"Coming!" a tingling voice replied from inside, then the lock turned and opened to reveal a teenager whose bright smile dimmed.

"Who are you?" she asked with a nervous frown.

"Who's there?" Okoko shouted from beyond the door.

She must have realized he was a threat and tried to close the door, but Rono used minimal effort to push her with the door and walked in with a bland smile.

Okoko's expectant gaze dimmed, just like his daughter's smile, when he saw who filled his doorway. His head and shoulders dropped forlornly, all signs of a guilty man who'd been caught.

Rono had expected he'd push away his food tray and wash his hands to better deal with him. But the older man just nodded at his daughter who proceeded to lock the door.

Okoko waved him to one of the leather seats on his left and continued eating. Trying to be brave, maybe.

"You might want your kid to retire for this," he suggested mildly.

The man had just shoved a piece of meat into his mouth, so he locked eyes with his kid and nodded at her. She hesitated, her eyes wide and swivelling from her dad to him and back to her dad. Rono could bet it was the shock of his deep voice, added to his overall looks, that cemented him a threat in the girl's mind. He stood at six feet, dark complexioned, with a pronounced head that didn't distract from his handsomeness and implied at first glance that he meant business.

When the kid had left, he settled on the settee and couldn't help the sigh that escaped from his mouth.

"Long day?"Okoko flicked him a contemplative gaze while licking his fingers.

"Depends on you." He turned, and caught him sighing.

"I didn't think you'd get here this soon."

Rono smiled though his eyes remained cold like shards of ice. "So, you're not denying it. I like that. I would like to get home early for once this week. Are you keeping her here?"

He looked around as though Felicia would be prodded forward from the alcove he sighted from his seat.

Okoko frowned in confusion. "Her who?"

"Honey?"

Both men turned to stare at the fidgeting woman—the daughter must have called her mother, his wife.

"Good evening, madam," Rono greeted courteously.

"Leave us alone!" Mrs. Okoko turned on him. His casual greeting had stoked her ire. "We don't want any trouble; we're not involved in—"

"Stella!"

Tears streamed down her face, and her sobs echoed in the room.

Okoko sighed. "It's alright, Stella. Go inside."

She hesitated like her daughter.

"Please don't kill my husband," she sobbed in a whisper, and Okoko groaned as though embarrassed.

In that moment, Rono wished he didn't have to kill Okoko. It shocked him every time he experienced a display of undying love between spouses, the kind his mother had never had for his father; the kind he wished he could find, which would translate to a happy family with more than one kid.

But that kind of love wasn't for a person like him, not after he'd drenched himself with the cloying stench of revenge. Surely, fate had overlooked him as a lost cause.

"Sweetheart, it's fine. Nobody is killing anybody … Go inside," he softly prodded, and she left.

"I see my reputation precedes me." Rono lifted his gaze from the marble floor to Okoko's face.

"I'm sorry about that. But you can excuse her fear at your presence in my home."

"I wouldn't be here if you hadn't kidnapped my girlfriend." Rono shrugged.

"Girlfriend?" Okoko sputtered."I don't even know her, and of what use would she be to me?"

"Good question. Answer that." He flicked open the button of his suit to better relax on the settee and grinned when Okoko's gaze swooped to the crimson stains on his shirt.

"Your father was good to me when he was—"

"Don't go there," he growled, smile disappearing.

"I'm saying that I keyed into your father's clean-up plan. I was a stooge for Umeh, but Ating still laid out the plan, explaining that we were too old to still be in the drug business. He spoke of a clean heritage for our kids."

"So why did your name pop up in my list as the sole brain behind Felicia's disappearance?"

"I presented my resignation before Jacob brought forward the idea of changing business lines. I paid the full price for withdrawing from The Table, a whooping nine-hundred-and-fifty-million naira. Right now, I feel like a fish out of water. I'm starting all over. I'll even have to sell my second house to get capital for the haulage business I want to start." Okoko's hands faced up, the food he'd been eating having dried up on his palm.

Rono turned to the silently playing TV. *Nine-hundred-and-fifty-million*, he pondered. He understood the price was that high because the men on The Table wanted to keep it contained. When one thought of the huge price, they'd reconsider withdrawing. And since it was on percentage, he worried his father's price would be in billions as he'd been a high stakes partner. He'd either have to continue in his place on The Table or pay the price.

The vibration of his phone broke the heavy silence. He pulled it from his suit pocket and frowned at the screen. Sighing, he answered. "What?"

"Have you found her?" Ekwere asked, his voice shaking.

"Wouldn't you have heard? I thought I asked you not to call me."

"I'm going to call the police. She went missing in your house," he threatened.

"Now, you're just pissing me off. I have a private investigator on it." He didn't want to involve the cops, not when he was of interest at the police headquarters after his father's death. "Besides, your daughter has pulled this stunt before, twice, actually."

"That's not what—"

"Have you forgotten so soon?"

"See, this—"

"The blame for your daughter's air-headedness is solely yours."

"Don't insult her that—"

"I'll advise you again. Don't call the cops without my consent; you won't like the consequences."

Rono ended the call and looked at the dumbfounded Okoko.

"Where were we?"

"I thought you said she was kidnapped?"

"This is where your name came up."

"I left The Table five months ago. It took three months to gather funds and pay the price. I've not attended a single meeting unless it concerned my withdrawal. I'm trying to cut ties with the underworld. Why would I sully that effort with kidnapping?"

"Maybe someone is trying to sully it for you."

Rono's offhand comment shocked Okoko for a moment—then, he looked up, eyes bright.

"I am sure The Table is worried about your vigilante … revenge rampage, and someone must be jittery."

Rono cocked his head. "It doesn't connect. I think my father was murdered for the throne as he had a greater chance of getting it."

"I didn't know that … but it coincides with him forcing a general change on The Table as president—"

Rono turned sharply. "He was president?"

Okoko nodded. "I'm surprised you didn't know. He eagerly signed off on my urge to leave The Table. It was his first act of office, and some people weren't happy about it."

"Who?"

The older man spewed names.

Rono's frown remained. "Pictures?"

Okoko nodded. "Stella!"

His wife stumbled out; it was obvious she hadn't returned to the room.

"Bring the photo album," he directed while lifting the basin of water to finally wash his hands. He was drying them on a towel when she resurfaced with a pack of pictures.

"I brought your glasses," she offered with shaky hands.

Rono saw the redness of her eyes and regretted being responsible for that. But a mission was a mission, and Felicia was still missing.

"Thanks, love," he said with an encouraging smile.

Rono soaked all of it and had to swallow a lump in his throat when the woman smiled lovingly at her husband despite the fear in her eyes.

Instead of leaving, she busied herself with lifting the food tray. By the time she returned to pick the water basin, Okoko had pulled out the photograph with all the Table members, including his father.

"It was the marriage of Umeh's daughter to an Assembly member at Anambra," he explained as Rono studied the smiling faces.

Okoko struggled out of his chair and moved closer. Rono perceived his meal on his breath, but was more focused on the photo.

"I assume this is Umeh." He pointed at a tall, fair-complexioned man dressed in red Ibo traditional attire.

Okoko nodded. "And that's his son beside him, Tony. He'd been quite bitter when your dad won over Umeh by a couple of votes."

"He's on The Table?"

"Yes."

Rono studied the men, all of his father's age group, late fifties and mid-sixties.

"I didn't know they allowed young people on The Table. I thought it was only through taking over from an existing member."

At least, that's what his father had told him when he'd insisted on joining in order to present alternative businesses The Table could run.

Okoko shrugged. "Umeh had begun bringing him for meetings without notice. Soon, the boy started contributing ideas, and nobody said anything."

Rono grunted and shoved the photograph into his suit pocket. He rose to his feet, towering over Okoko who struggled to his feet only to bend backwards to see his face.

"Thank you, sir, for your information."

He walked towards the door. It appeared this whole situation was more complicated than he'd thought. Someone was trying to cover his tracks by kidnapping Felicia—he had to watch everybody closely. Even Okoko wasn't off the hook yet.

"Accept my sympathy on your father's demise, and—"

He turned to the older man. "Yes?"

Okoko fidgeted. "It might be nothing, but your father had mentioned in an offhand comment how Tony Umeh seemed to always compare himself with you whenever he mentioned your strides in a conversation."

Rono slid his hand into his suit flap again and brought out a complimentary card. "In case you hear anything. Thank you."

It was obvious his dad had been hiding things from him. He had to find those things and place them side by side with the ones he'd discovered already. He was close—his gut told him so—but something was really off.

His phone vibrated again. He nodded at Okoko, opened his door, and stepped outside before answering the call.

"You can go home, Sly. I trust you did a good job."

CHAPTER THREE

Police

It sounded like the shriek of a dying man in his sleep, but it was only the archaic doorbell his father had insisted on using. Sometimes, Rono thought his father had left the nerve-rattling bell just to piss him off.

He rolled onto his back, sighing when the bell shrieked again. His excuse for that thing still surviving was his being busy preparing to bury his dad, the funeral event, and now, the investigation.

He missed him.

They'd not always been on the same page, but he was his dad; he'd loved him fiercely. He'd believed every decision he took would be with the hope of a positive future consequence to benefit his only son.

Sighing and feeling the depression from not being sure who to focus his vengeance on next, Rono glanced at his dad's photograph and pondered going to his own house. But then, he shook his head. That decision would entail shopping for furniture and making the place habitable. He'd just remain here as he'd always done whenever in town.

"What the hell?" he growled at the shrieking bell. "It's Sunday, for crying out loud, shouldn't it be quiet around here?" he groused as he pulled on a plain white T-shirt over grey suede pants.

Padding barefoot downstairs, he crossed the huge parlour and opened the door to ... cops.

He frowned in confusion. "Can I help you?"

His tone was respectful even though the uniformed men seemed in awe of him. That could happen when you were assigned to arrest the son of a business magnate, a pillar of society, and royalty, too, while standing in front of his palatial residence. He would get away with pulling the prince rank on them; they were expecting him to, but he wouldn't.

"Mr. Ating." A plain clothes cop who'd had his back to him turned.

"Ah, Detective Etuk. Good morning; is this about my father's case?"

Etuk shook his head with a strained smile. "This is about your girlfriend, Felicia Ekwere. Do you know her whereabouts?"

Rono arranged his face to show concern. "Isn't she with her dad?"

Etuk pinned him with a knowing look. "You'll have to come with us to the station for questioning. You've been accused of knowing about her disappearance."

One of the uniformed men promptly dangled a pair of handcuffs.

If looks could kill, the cop would be dangling by his neck.

"No need for that." His tone remained mild while his gaze could've frozen a lake. "I'll follow you willingly."

"Thank you."

Etuk sighed and nodded when he asked to get a pair of slippers.

"I took the liberty of brushing," he announced, stepping out in the same clothes but with comfortable slip-ons, his phone, and keys.

"Sir?"

Rono turned from locking the door to find his driver and smiled calmly at him.

"Don't look alarmed. It's about Felicia. I'm just following them for questioning. Call Uncle Timothy and bring the car to the headquarters."

He walked beside Etuk, and the uniformed cops followed like security escorts.

***

"This is my colleague, Detective Ukor. He'll be sitting in on the questioning." Etuk waved at the man, whose disdain for Rono couldn't be more obvious.

Rono nodded at the man and returned his gaze to his phone, muting it before dropping it on their scarred table and focusing on them.

"How long has she been missing?"

"I had no idea she'd been missing, Detective Etuk. I simply assumed she'd returned to her father's house."

"So, how long have you assumed this?"

"Over a week."

"Did you call or text to find out if indeed she was there?"

Rono shook his head.

"So, because you're some kind of prince, you don't value other people's safety." The venom in Ukor's tone couldn't be mistaken.

Rono gave him a wide eyed stare and turned the same expression on Etuk.

"I think we better wait for my lawyer," he suggested calmly, causing Etuk to glare at his partner, whose disdain increased.

In the awkward silence that followed, his phone vibrated. "Yes, Abel."

"I've called Uncle Timothy over twenty times; he's not answering his calls. What should I do?"

The driver seemed really worried. Rono would have called the other lawyers his father had on retainer, but he was trying to keep this close to the vest.

"Keep trying."

"Alright, sir."

When he dropped his phone, he looked at Etuk with the haughtiness only a prince could convey. "In the absence of my lawyer, seeing as he's suddenly become a Christian and is probably at church, I will overlook this whole drama and the insult it smears on my person because I believe you're just doing your jobs. So, I'll tell you what I know."

The atmosphere had changed with his attitude. Etuk swallowed with difficulty, and Ukor tried to look unaffected, but his incessant twitch on his chair gave away his nervousness and fear for having insulted royalty.

"Felicia was just a girlfriend for appearances. Truth be told, she was a pest to me—"

"So you had her killed … kidnapped?" Ukor interrupted, his disdain still obvious.

Rono ignored him. "Our relationship was a prodding by our fathers; we weren't compatible. Felicia is a dunce, to put it mildly, and I like women with a bit of sense. I know you wouldn't understand that, Detective Ukor, but it's okay."

Etuk's lips twitched furiously at the mild barb, and he lowered his head to hide his smile while his partner sputtered angrily.

"Is there a point to this, Mr. Ating?"

"Of course. I'd made it known to Felicia that I'm not interested in having even casual sex with her. That'd be a waste of my swimmers—"

"Swimmers? Who are these swimmers?" Ukor exploded.

Rono smiled. "That will be my sperm, Detective. Sleeping with her would've been a waste of my sperm. Again, I get your confusion."

Etuk cleared his throat loudly. "Right …"

"Felicia didn't like hearing that. She kept throwing herself at me. I only tolerated her because I was staying at my father's house. Treating her badly would invite a harangue from my dad. I have been ignoring her for as long as she's been trying to get my attention.

"She's done this kind of thing before. The first time was in December 2015, two months after we'd met. She was staying over at the house, but my driver noticed she hadn't returned from her shopping spree by midnight. I reported it to the police and was extremely embarrassed when she returned the next morning, smelling like a distillery, with the only excuse that she was bored."

Etuk shook his head and wrote on his jotter.

"Last year, about June, when I was in the country and had to reiterate that I wasn't interested in a relationship no matter how casual, she disappeared for three days, and my dad's security detail was extremely worried and reported it to the police since I'd left town for a bit."

"It seems to me you were preparing for a day like this, seeing as you have all your dates ready." Ukor sneered.

"I won't apologise for being smart, Detective."

"Did you have a disagreement with her or anything that would make her react like this?"

Rono shook his head. "No, I ignored her as usual. I didn't have the time for her drama. My father was murdered," he snapped, sitting up and allowing reign of his anger.

Etuk sighed. "I—"

"How's this difficult to see? Can't you detect the yearly drama she's acting? 2015, 2016, and now 2017? My father was murdered in November. I had to handle his business, the royal traditions, the legal issues, the company, the funeral arrangements ... everything! I'm still neck deep in figuring out contracts, agreements, royal matters—" Not to talk of the scary wait for the impending summons from The Table. "—so forgive me if I have no time for a girl that wasn't even my girlfriend."

He paused for effect here.

"And this begs the question. What *is* going on with my dad's case?"

***

Hours later, Etuk had to explain that Felicia's best friend, one Suzie Udoma, was responsible for the report that got him to the station.

Rono's phone vibrated. When he looked, Dave's name flashed. His throat constricted—he hadn't heard from him by four a.m. as they'd agreed. He would've called him, but Dave had always warned him not to call when he was in the field.

He ignored the call.

"Do you know her?"

"No."

His phone vibrated again; he hoped Dave was okay. His cousin had been with him every step in his vendetta and had been responsible for handling the selloff of his father's drug cache at Eastern Obolo, an island community sharing a boundary with Rivers State. It was a dangerous operation, seeing as his father had died arranging it.

Dave had agreed to go—he was more experienced in the field part of things and had been his father's muscle from his immediate post-teen years. As a cousin from his mother's side, Dave had pestered his father to work for him so that he could take care of his younger siblings. Despite Rono's mother abandoning her family, and Dave's father, her brother, being a drunk, Chief Jacob Ating had still taken him in and insisted he attain some level of education.

Rono got the feeling that Dave hadn't really been interested in school. He'd grudgingly done it, attending a polytechnic instead of university.

While Etuk tried to explain the investigation on his father's case without revealing too much, Dave called thrice more, and Etuk gave up the subtle glances and looked Rono in the face.

"You can answer Dave's call, you know," he suggested. He knew Dave was his cousin.

Rono smiled. "Continue, please."

The detective huffed. "Anyway, we spoke with the other contender for the throne, Chief Akodi, and he explained the selection process for the throne. Usually, the four royal families took turns ruling until death. This contention between the Ating and Akodi royal families came as a result of Akodi family being passed over in your great-grandfather's time because they'd not had a son at the time, so the crown came to Ating.

"The crown has rotated again, and it should be Ating's turn, but the Akodi family feel slighted and are demanding their right. The king makers will decide after due consultations, and Chief Akodi made me understand that killing your father for the throne would be useless because, if the crown comes to Ating royal family, you'll be chosen as your dad had no brothers."

Rono nodded calmly, but inside, fear pattered. He already knew what the detective had found out. Some family elders had explained it to him during preparations for his dad's funeral, and they'd been stern when he'd declared his disinterest with the throne.

Dave's name flashed on the screen again, and Rono knew something was terribly wrong. It didn't show on his face, but he was impatient to leave.

"So, are we done here?"

"I think so. We'll reach out if anything else comes up in both cases. Don't leave the state, though."

He sighed. "Right."

He got to his feet, nodded at the detective, and walked out of his office.

When he stepped outside and scanned the parking lot for Abel, his eyes caught and held those of Felicia's supposed best friend. She ducked her head to avoid his gaze while having a heated discussion with Detective Ukor.

He'd not recognized her name, but he knew Suzie well—she'd been with Felicia during his father's funeral. But like everything about Felicia, he'd ignored her.

Lowering her gaze from his and rubbing her neck uncomfortably in a bid to hide her face, expressed guilt—she mustn't have acted alone. Felicia's idiot father must have sent her. Did the old man think he wouldn't know?

"Sir ..."

"Where are you parked, Abel?" he asked, reading Dave's SMS about a betrayal at the selloff and having found Felicia even though she was chubby now.

Rono frowned, deleted the message, and waited to enter his car before calling Dave.

"Close to the gate, sir."

He looked to where he'd pointed and saw Uncle Timothy driving into the station.

"What was his excuse?"

"Nothing. He just said he'd get here as soon as possible."

"How long ago was that?" he muttered, schooling his face to relief as they neared Timothy's car.

"Over three hours ago, sir," Abel whispered.

"Uncle Timothy, I'm sorry to have disturbed you. It was nothing; everything is sorted out. The detective apologised. It could have been something casually handled not brought to the station, but they were just doing their jobs, so …"

"Oh, I'm sorry I took time." The robust, middle-aged man smiled thinly; no explanations as to what had kept him came forth.

And Rono wasn't going to ask.

"Okay, I'm out of here. I apologise for the wasted time, again."

"You seem in such a hurry," Timothy commented, widening his car door but not entering it.

Rono grinned. "I'm going to church."

"At this time?" He checked his wrist watch, a shiny gold Rolex, quite unusual for the reserved lawyer he'd known all his life. "It's past four p.m."

Rono gave him another smile. "I know. It's the perfect time for confession."

CHAPTER FOUR

Ekwere's Compound

When the strange giant Paapa had brought to the clinic—Dave—had called her 'Felicia', Suto Ekwere had frozen and swallowed non-existent saliva several times before she could make her voice sound unperturbed.

In that ungodly hour, she'd reaffirmed the importance of skill expertise. Her mind had been racing a mile a second and to different directions while she'd sutured the bullet wounds. Who was he; why was he at Eastern Obolo; what was going on?

She'd been glad for her timely transfer, and instead of returning home the next day as planned, she'd packed up the moment Paapa had left the premises. She had dreaded working at the metropolis, but after that morning, she'd tried to be glad about going home.

The gladness vanished when her father opened the door with a question.

"Suto … what are you doing here?" His eyes had widened like a kid caught at a naughty act.

The dread suffused her chest again—there really was something fishy going on.

"I'm looking for my sugar daddy, what do you think?" She rolled her eyes and pushed through the door he'd been hesitant to fully open.

Ekwere chuckled nervously. "You know what I mean, sweetie. You never leave that rustic village even for the holidays, and you're always on about saving lives and doing good. So, it's a shock to find you at the door with no *prior* notice."

Suto didn't miss the emphasis on prior, and her father never called her sweetie. She narrowed her eyes at him. "Okay, what's going on?"

He blinked in quick succession. "How do you mean, darling?"

Her mouth dropped ... Two endearments in one minute? It must be worse than she'd imagined. Nodding to herself, she made a snap decision.

"Okay, Father. I don't know what you've gotten yourself into this time, and I don't want to know. I'll stay at your house as long as it takes me to lobby my transfer to somewhere else. I don't want to be dragged into whatever is going on. That said, is there food in the house?"

"Did you drop a maid when you left?"

There's the father she knew; the charge and bail lawyer who could sell his child just to dupe a business partner or client, the one who encouraged prostitution if he'd benefit from it. His response had eradicated the jittery urge to return home and possibly save the day. Her father would remain dubious 'til death.

Suto shrugged, hefted her huge carryall, and walked into the corridor that led to her room.

***

Rono had not been lying when he'd told Timothy he was going to church, but it'd not only been for confessions.

Abel had rolled into the church premises, found a parking spot, and left the car for his phone call.

"Why did you get arrested?" Dave had barked moments on the call.

Rono had understood his anxiety. His cousin, older than him by a couple of years, had assumed the role of elder brother from the moment his father had taken him in as a son.

"I was invited to talk, not arrested."

"Same difference. They could've talked at your home. If you reached the station, it was an arrest."

Rono had sighed. He enjoyed his cousin's over protectiveness, but not at the moment. "You didn't call at four a.m."

"I got shot."

His heart had jumped into his throat, and before he could chastise him, Dave had told him all that had happened.

At first, Dave had thought the drug lord from Rivers had double-crossed him. The man had trust issues and had insisted that Dave stay back until the merchandise had crossed to the other side of the river.

It hadn't been a problem for Dave, but unbeknownst to the Rivers man, he'd arranged to return the money to town. With the help of the old man, Paapa, whose compound had been used for the exchange, Dave and two of the four boys he'd brought from town, the other two having gone in search of food, had wrapped the money in sacks of rotten fish and had hired some village women to pose as traders returning from purchasing bags of fish, all to avoid police inspection on the road to Uyo.

It had turned out good that the other two hadn't been around, so when they'd returned, Dave had given them transport to go home. But unknown to him, one of them, Mkpouto, hadn't. So, while Rono had been waiting for Dave's call at four a.m., his cousin had been running for his life in the waterfront forest of Eastern Obolo.

Mkpouto had returned with two other thugs, requesting the money. Dave had dived into the forest while they shot at him, and when he'd thought he'd surely die, the old man, Paapa, had appeared with his sons and saved him with their hunting rifles. Dave had fainted from blood loss, and then, he'd woken at a maternity clinic where a now chubby Felicia had operated on his gunshot wound.

That, Rono didn't understand. More confusing was Dave's obvious sensual interest in this chubby Felicia, when his cousin had hated her more than him. But that wasn't the problem.

"So, Mkpouto is dead?" He'd felt sorry for the young boy even though he'd chosen to betray them.

"He'd told the old man's son a lawyer had contracted some other dude to double-cross me, not the Rivers man, and he'd been chosen for a huge fee to be the inside guy. Fortunately, he'd left to find food before I'd changed my mind and asked that the money still proceed to town while I wait."

Rono had sighed. It appeared the line of betrayal kept widening even after his father's death, and a lawyer was involved—who might it be?

"Why are we speaking on the phone?"

"I wonder, man. I'm in position already, counting and storing, I'll see you after confession."

Dave had been storing money, and the position he'd been talking about was an empty tomb in the corner of the priests' cemetery at the St. Joseph Catholic Church, Anua.

When they'd met, the storing had been complete, and Rono had been unable to stop himself from hugging his cousin. He'd groaned in pain as the hug had affected his wounded left shoulder, but he had hugged him back and then shifted him aside to tell him more about Felicia.

That had been two days ago. He'd given himself time to plan the perfect revenge for the scheming old fart and to find out what the hell was going on with Felicia having a double ... if that was real; Dave might have been hallucinating from the pain or the drugs he'd been given. There was no way Felicia, thin as bone and dumb as sheep, was suddenly chubby and a doctor. Dave insisted he'd crushed on her when in reality, Dave hated Felicia more than he did.

Dave: He's home...just got back

Dave had decided to stake out Ekwere's compound, a huge, fenced round building which was probably an inheritance—it looked old-fashioned enough—and located off Nwaniba Road, on an untarred street, almost close to Le Meridien, the five-star hotel.

Rono: Right. I'm going in. Stay woke though, in case I need help hanging him from the balls

He stepped down from his car parked three houses from Ekwere's compound and strolled towards it, buttoning his grey suit over a white shirt. He grinned at the laughing smiley Dave had sent and waited just inside the gate for the reply he was typing.

*Dave: You have a silencer, man. Just shoot his balls and be done with it ^eye-roll smiley^*

Rono: Lol. Deleting...
Dave: Be safe...deleted

They'd decided not to keep any messages on their phones. Rono had learnt a lot of security hacks from security courses he'd decided to do while at Birmingham, during his doctorate. He only texted Dave, and they always deleted at the end of every chat.

Movement caught his eye on the far right side of the compound. A sparse garden spread out with low-height fruit trees in the periphery of his gaze, but his eyes seemed to zero in on the fair-skinned, chubby woman stretching up to pluck a fruit. In the process, black markings peeked out from under her shirt.

Rono wasn't a fan of tattoos. He'd never consciously go for a chubby woman, and he disliked skimpy dressing. But the instant, visceral reaction he had at the sight of the plump woman in a short jean skirt and a tattoo on her right hip seemed to erase all he'd thought he believed.

Everything appeared to fade, and the unknown woman gleamed as she stood on tiptoe to pluck a fruit. Her rounded buttocks, a siren that called to him, and her fair, full legs made him salivate.

The vibration in his pocket broke the trance, startling him into marching to Ekwere's front door, earlier described by Dave.

"What the fuck just happened?" he muttered, shaking his head and breathing deeply to slow his palpitating heart. He'd never had such a reaction to a woman, and he'd not even seen her face.

He had a pressing urge to go back and see her face. His heart pounded as his designer shoe-covered feet began retracing his steps ...

"What are you doing?" he snapped, annoyed with himself, and rushed back to Ekwere's front door which stood slightly open.

Looking around, he was glad Ekwere's neighbours lived upstairs, thus making him safe from prying eyes as he pulled his gun, hiding it behind him, and widened the door.

His last thought as he located Ekwere, lounging on his sofa, was returning at a later date to seek the elusive chubby, tattoo-wielding woman.

When the man looked up, saw him, and rushed for his phone on the coffee table, all other concerns drained from Rono's body, leaving his usual cold and detached self. He pointed the gun at the terrified middle-aged man and shook his head, silently glad that the earlier strange feeling had evaporated. If he killed Ekwere today, he wasn't ever coming back this way, siren tenant or not.

"Sit back, old man," he directed, picked up Ekwere's phone, and shoved it into his pocket. "This can go fast and smooth, or torturous and long. Depends on you."

Rono watched him swallow with difficulty, and that's how he noticed his eyes become shifty and a sneer crawl up his weathered face.

"You cannot kill me. People will hear the shot."

How stupid was this man? And how had his father ever thought to have business dealings with him? "Seriously, that's your safety net?"

Ekwere flinched under the cold, calm stare Rono sent him. If the man were smart, he'd recall some of the things Jacob must have told him about his son's character, plus the rumours of killings. He shifted when Rono sat beside him, both of them facing the front door.

"Some—Someone might walk in ..."

"Hmm," Rono grunted in agreement.

Without hurry, he slid his hand into the flap of his suit, bringing out a rolled up leather pouch which he flipped. When it rolled open, Ekwere gasped at the array of shiny steel in several tiny pockets. Before he could blink, another device had left Rono's suit flap.

With great care, he lifted the knives from their pockets, laying them on top of the pouch, then he placed the muzzle-like device with the knives.

"That's a silencer. People won't hear. And having realized I've not locked your door after shutting it, the knives are for whoever walks through that door."

Ekwere whimpered, real fear settling in his eyes as he realized Rono wasn't joking.

"I'm … I'm so … so … sorry." Sweat dripped down his face, soaking up his white, lawyer's shirt.

"For what, Barrister?" Rono crossed his right leg over his left in a comfortable posture. He allowed his gun hand to rest beside the knives on his right, conveniently pointing at Ekwere.

At his simple question, the man's eyes darted from left to right. Rono could see the wheels turning in his mind as he tried to figure out what he must know.

His plan was to keep him unbalanced while getting unquestioned answers from him.

"I warned you this will happen if you brought in the cops."

"But … but … I didn't …"

"Where is Felicia?"

Ekwere licked his lips, his eyes rapidly blinking as if he thought to lie.

Rono reacted instinctively when the front door opened. His gun flew to his left hand while his right picked a knife and threw, timing it well enough to only nick the arm of the intruder … who happened to be the fruit plucking siren out-front—he'd never forget her figure and snug skirt.

"What the fuck?" she screamed, bending over and letting go her of bunched up T-shirt, scattering the guavas she'd been carrying on the tiled floor as her right palm slapped over the wound on her arm.

"Close and lock the door," Rono directed, the gun back to his right hand but now pointed at her.

None of the other occupants of the room knew his heart slammed like a jack hammer against his chest from instant remorse at marring her smooth skin.

Ekwere had gotten over his whimpers, his eyes wide as he stared at the siren lady who did as directed before raising her face for the first time.

"That's … that's Felicia," the older man blurted in a jubilant tone.

"What?"

Rono frowned with his head cocked to the side, his own show of disbelief. Ekwere must want to die today—the man couldn't stop lying.

"It's her … Can't you see? Felicia, tell him," he prodded with the fakest smile ever expressed.

Even if she'd not exclaimed, he'd have known the blatant lie. It was as though he was staring at Felicia but not Felicia. Twins, he figured, but their resemblance ended at the face and complexion.

This one was tall, probably five-foot-six, full-figured, with eyes gleaming intelligence … She must be the doctor Dave crushed on.

Rono refused to think about his earlier reaction to her outside. He identified the heaving of her considerable bosom and narrowed eyes spitting fury at her father.

"Take a seat. Your father was just about to tell me where your sister is."

Her father sputtered in mock indignation. Concern shadowed her eyes, and she hesitated before moving to the seat backing the front door.

"Tell him!" Ekwere snapped in a fierce whisper at his daughter.

Rono followed all her moves, unable to look away or stop the palpitation of his heart. When she pulled her palm from the wound to stare at the blood, he tightened his jaw to control the reflex to rush to her side. He breathed better upon noticing the blood had clotted, but guilt remained a live thing in his chest.

When she looked up, her eyes were defiant. "I don't know what this is about, and I don't care, but I don't want to be a part of it. I'm not Felicia."

While she spoke, Ekwere twitched on his seat as though ants crawled in his pants. His gaze could've killed her if they were weapons.

"Ahem," Rono started.

Ekwere turned to him, jittery all over.

"I recently found out the total amount of your debt to my dad which you should've paid off five months ago," he continued. "Should I assume you murdered my father to get away from paying … twenty-two million naira?"

His daughter gasped with widened eyes focused on her guilty father.

***

Twenty-two million naira! What would her dad want with that kind of money, and how did Felicia figure into this drama? Was this tied to the giant she'd treated at Eastern Obolo a few days ago? Was this why he'd said they'd been looking for Felicia?

And where *was* Felicia?

After deciding to ignore whatever trouble her father and twin had obviously gotten into again, she'd refused to ask her father about Felicia's whereabouts. Asking would've resulted in discovering the problem, and she would've been forced, as always, to find solutions, which would involve money. Because no matter how many times she got furious with her dad and twin every time they got into trouble, she still had not been able to abandon them.

But twenty-two million naira was more than they could chew. She'd have to save over ten years of her salary to pay back, and this man would not wait that long. She could see this just by looking at his stoic face.

Despite his cold eyes, she worried that in a different situation, she'd have fallen for this guy. It was rare to find men this dark with pink lips and brown eyes like contacts outside a foreign music video. Even though he sat, she could see he was tall. His thighs had bulk, and in between …

Her father's stammers broke her trance. Shame suffused her chest at the direction of her thoughts. Instead of worrying for her family or being terrified of the gunman, she was crushing on him.

"God forbid! I would never," Ekwere sputtered, his eyes flashing truth for the first time.

"I want the money, then."

"I will ... Well, I need some time to ... to source the money."

The young man picked up the silencer and slowly twisted it on the muzzle of his gun without looking up.

Suto's heart stuttered. Her father's mouth dropped in shock, but her gaze remained riveted on the measured movements of the gunman. He was the most unemotional person she'd ever met; yet, she shivered with an emotion that wasn't entirely fear.

Ekwere's breathing came in pants. "You cannot do that ..."

"I've been here for almost an hour," he began as though having a casual conversation. "And I've gained nothing."

He picked up a knife, stared at it, seeming to reconsider, then picked the next one. Suto could perceive her father's terror, and it bled into her chest, causing a tightening in her throat.

"You've not told me where Felicia is, why I was arrested, and when I'll be getting my money."

"But ... bu—"

"You're the doctor."

It took Suto a while to realize he'd spoken to her. She met his cold gaze and nodded. It hadn't been a question.

Stretching, the man laid the knife on her father's arm, in the juncture of the elbow. "How long will it take him to bleed to death if I slash his brachial artery, right here?"

He tapped the spot despite her father's wild eyes and shivering torso.

Suto couldn't find her voice. Her mouth dropped, her eyes widened. "You wouldn't ... Please ..."

"Answer the question."

She swallowed, every other emotion but terror draining from her. "Without pressure, it'll take two to three minutes."

The man turned to her father, who shifted to the edge of the couch but couldn't escape the cold steel of the knife. "That's how long you have to talk or die."

His wrist flicked, and blood bloomed on the arm of the white shirt, spreading at an alarming rate.

Suto screamed and made to rush to her father who was choking on his words, but the man pointed the gun at her and slowly shook his head.

"Talk, Daddy!" she cried.

"I faked Felicia's kidnap to get ransom money from you. And—and then pay you with it when and if you asked for your father's debt."

Despite the crawling terror in her chest, Suto knew her father would've left town with the money; a flicker in the gun-man's eyes told her he knew it, too.

"My arrest?"

"Just part of the plan ..."

"My money?"

Her father paused and licked his lips, his eyes shifting to land on Suto, then back to the man. "Take her as a wife!"

"What? Daddy!" she burst out.

The man's eyes narrowed. "I couldn't stand Felicia. What makes you think—"

"Because The Table is making a new rule just for you. As an unmarried man, you can't speak at The Table or even claim your father's interests ..."

"How do you know The Table? Besides, Tony Umeh joins the meetings."

"Tony Umeh is engaged and planning a wedding." At this, his head lolled to the side, his eyelids dropping.

"Please, let me help him." Her voice shook.

He simply nodded as she slammed her knees on the floor beside her dad and tore the arm of the shirt. When she looked closely, she realized he hadn't nicked the deadly brachial artery, but it was a wide gash, nonetheless. The heavy bleeding resulted from her father's anxiety which spiked his heart rate, thereby producing more blood.

Had it been a mistake, or had he avoided the artery on purpose?

Suto shook her head, swallowing as she put pressure on her father's wound. She was just grateful it wasn't deadly.

"How do you know so much?" the man broke into her father's moans.

The older man turned weakly and, upon seeing him still holding a knife, he swallowed, dropped his gaze, and replied, "He's engaged to Felicia."

CHAPTER FIVE

Ewet Housing Estate

Suto barely noticed the high rise neighbourhood as the tricycle whisked her to the gunman's house—it was how she called him in her head, though she now knew his name was Rono Ating.

Her heart hammered as she wondered if she was doing the right thing. Her dad, for the first time in his life, had been altruistic and asked her to leave town. She'd asked him what would happen to him and Felicia if she did, and he'd said they'd die.

She now knew her sister was engaged to Tony Umeh for a marriage of convenience because her father also owed his father, and the Umehs had no idea Felicia was a twin.

No matter how she hated the situation and dreaded marrying a cold-blooded killer, she didn't want her only family dead. So, she'd gotten his number and set an appointment for three p.m.

***

"What has marriage got to do with it? I feel he's lying, and he could be the lawyer Mkpouto had talked about before death," Dave insisted.

He'd said the same thing the previous day when Rono had recounted the happenings at Ekwere's house.

"Anybody can pose as a lawyer. I believe him because Uncle Timothy confirmed that Dad's interest was in billions. I need to join The Table and investigate these people. They could be in on the conspiracy to kill Dad."

"But ... But you can find someone else, Ron. It mustn't be her. I'm in love with her." Dave pouted.

Rono rolled his eyes. "You're in love with a lot of girls."

"Not like this one. Besides, I saw her first."

"Oh, it's like that now?" His eyes widened. "Okay, her father gave her to me."

He smirked.

"I'm not letting her go without a fight," Dave warned, flexing his muscles.

Rono smiled, looking away from his cousin. They were different as day and night; Dave was fair, bulky, loved to party, was more forgiving, and barked more than bit. While he was dark, not as bulky, didn't party, was vengeful, bit more than he barked, and stood some inches shorter than Dave. Yet, they shared an unbreakable bond that was more than blood.

This was the first time they were having a clash of interest.

"See, I don't even like her ..." His heart twisted at the fib.

"Exactly, find someone else—"

"But this is necessary. She knows stuff and is willing to help."

"It's not you. She's helping her father who owes you twenty-two mill—"

The doorbell shrieked, echoing in the vast house. They knew who was at the door, and so stared at each other and bolted for the library door at the same time.

Dave won by shoving Rono off using his bulk and punching him on the shoulder for good measure. Rono bent over, groaning when he shut him in the library, then raced to the front door while straightening his shirt and smiled when Dave opened the door.

***

Suto knew she looked like a rabbit caught in headlights upon seeing who opened the door. This spiked her anxiety and made breathing difficult.

"Hey, there, beautiful. Remember me?"

How could she forget?

"Err ... How's your ... wound?" She reverted to doctor mode—safer this way.

He waved her in, shut the door, and pulled up his T-shirt to show off the small scar. That was when Rono walked in.

Oh, God, why was this happening to her? The giant was handsome, and his upper body looked better when he was standing up. They'd make a beautiful couple, but she didn't have the shivers for him. Not like the ones she had the moment the gunman walked in.

His mien wasn't expressionless as she recalled—he seemed pissed, and with good reason: his prospective wife stared at his friend's sexy chest.

"Sit," he grunted after they'd both escorted her in.

She sighed and moved towards the couch, since he'd taken a single seat. An awkward silence ensued when Dave walked out of the sitting room.

"I, err ..." she began, tired of waiting for him to say something, like welcome her, at least. "I understand the marriage will be beneficial to you, so, I'd do it to offset Father's debt, and when all is settled, we could get a divorce."

Why was he frowning so much now? She'd have expected him to have liked such a straightforward agreement.

"Here, sweetheart." The giant—Dave—returned, handing her a glass of juice.

She flashed him a relieved smile, a break from the stifling tension. She thanked him and took a sip, forcing it down through her tightened throat.

"So, I'd planned to come see you to pull the sutures." Dave smiled widely, sitting close to her.

Rono frowned even more. She'd even say he looked like he was fighting the urge to drag his cousin from her side and punch him for good measure.

"Those were cosmetic ones. They melt."

***

Rono let out a breath of relief and hardened his jaw because he didn't know why he was relieved that she wouldn't be seeing or touching Dave's naked chest, medical capacity or not.

"Oh, I'd never imagine such a small clinic would have that." Dave sounded genuinely surprised.

"I have a personal stash."

"Now, why do you have a personal stash of medical supplies?" Dave wriggled his eyebrows at her.

She smiled. "And what were you doing at Eastern Obolo?"

"Touché," Rono murmured, not knowing he'd spoken out in his pride for her—she gave as hard as she took, this woman.

"Did you say something, Ron?"

They'd both turned to stare.

"Can I speak with you in the library?" he asked his cousin.

They had a mini face-off before Dave sighed and followed him.

"You're interfering," he accused.

"Of course I am."

"She wants to marry me! She said so!" His whisper came out vehement. *She's mine,* he almost growled, not understanding the territorial feeling building in his chest for her.

"If you cancelled her father's debt, she wouldn't have to."

"I can't do that."

"You can't, or you won't."

Rono huffed—he didn't know what he was doing anymore. Truth be told, his present urge was to forget everything and concentrate on this girl like a normal guy would. But he'd invested so much in finding his dad's killers, and he didn't know how to let go.

He licked his lips, trying but unable to tell his cousin that he liked the doctor. He cleared his throat and brought out his ATM card.

"You can furnish the house now." He slapped the thin plastic on Dave's chest.

"You're suddenly willing, after all this time? You just want me out of the house." Dave grinned and walked out. "But it's a good bribe," he flung over his shoulder.

Rono sighed in relief and followed him, but his breath stilled again when Dave bent and kissed her cheek. To her credit, she started and almost spilled her drink on her beautiful Ankara trouser and top.

"I'll be seeing you around, honey," his cousin enthused and walked out of the house.

Rono had never wanted to harm the man as he did then.

Now that he was alone with her, he realized he was now responsible for making her comfortable ... something he'd never been good at. He had always been straightforward in relationships as he'd never found anyone he wanted to be nice to. Most of the girls were after his money and lacked the brain capacity to sustain an intelligent conversation, so he'd done one-night-stands when necessary. He hated that he couldn't be as jovial as Dave, that he couldn't make her smile.

He cleared his throat and retook his seat. "Sorry about that."

"Your friend is a storm." She smiled.

Her smile was absolutely lovely, but it had still been for Dave. Would she ever smile for him, especially after he'd forced her into a marriage of convenience?

"He's my cousin," he blurted out. "Not that he isn't my friend, but I just wanted to clarify—" He choked and paused to clear his throat.

Suto's eyes widened. "Oh."

So much weight in those two letters. Had she figured out he'd grown nervous around her?

"Fuck," he murmured. "I'm sorry about yesterday. Is your dad okay?"

He'd never ever apologised for his actions.

She frowned. "Yes, he's fine."

Awkward silence filled the room.

"You look nice," he stammered, and cringed at the fact that he sounded weak.

He sounded like a person he'd despise, actually.

She looked horrified, as if she, too, were having the same thought.

Rono read her expression, regretting his words, but he didn't know how to retract them without being an asshole, and for once in his life, he was worried about being an asshole.

As the tension in the vast sitting room built, breathing became difficult. He murmured an excuse and rushed to his feet in a bid to escape the room.

"Wait!" She dropped her drink and stood, moving to where he'd stopped.

When she looked in his eyes, everything disappeared from his mind. Whatever she'd thought to say also seemed to have vanished as she stood there before him with her mouth open.

Her eyes closed halfway, as if with longing, and then, she lowered her gaze to his lips. His heart rate spiked. Would she ...

Suto closed the small space, pulled his head down, and softly locked lips with him. Upon that first contact, she moaned and then darted her tongue as if to taste him.

Everything else fell to the wayside, and Rono stood there momentarily numb, his arms hanging lamely while the strangest and most delicious feeling suffused his entire body. He was revelling in this feeling when it seemed as though she'd withdraw, and why shouldn't she when he'd just stood there?

He grabbed her waist, pulled her closer, aligning her softness to his hardness, and ravaged her mouth in the deepest kiss he'd ever given. Her moan sent thrills of pleasure shooting through his body straight to his groin.

A grunt escaped when his hand slid under her top, feeling the softest skin. He flexed his hips against her belly, causing both of them to moan ...

What the hell were they doing?

The thought made him snatch his lips from hers and step back, breathing as hard as she was, her lips so swollen, he wanted nothing else but to get back there.

"At least, we have chemistry, so the marriage shouldn't be so bad," she huffed.

Was it embarrassment that made her lower her head, or was she checking out the obvious bulge in his trousers?

"Fuck," he muttered and dropped his hands over his groin.

But then, his phone rang, so he settled for pushing her away gently before pulling out his phone.

Why did she now sport such a silly smile on her beautiful face?

"Hey, Uncle Timothy," he answered, trying to get past the log in his throat.

"The Table reached out to me as your father's attorney and extended an invitation to you."

Cold doused him upon hearing these words. He listened while wondering about the sudden invitation and why it'd taken so long. He'd buried his dad in January, and this was April. He didn't want to be controlled by these people; he would go there on his own terms.

"I can't do that, Uncle," he interrupted the lawyer.

"Do you know … Why?" he sputtered.

Rono turned and locked gazes with Suto, enjoying how she bit her lower lip. "I'm getting married."

CHAPTER SIX

De-Castle Luxury Home
She'd kissed him. What in God's name had possessed her to do that? She was usually controlled, unlike her sister who embarrassed herself for men. But she'd yearned to find out if his pink lips were as soft as they looked ... and then, when she'd tasted that hint of whiskey on them, Heaven.

Dear God, she had initiated a kiss with the gunman; a man she should be terrified of, a man she should be pissed at for her dilemma ... Okay, her dad was responsible for the dilemma, but the gunman was going along with it.

Suto stood there, analysing her feelings while he made another phone call. Her eyes followed his pacing, lingering on the strength of his arms and hands—she swallowed with difficulty—hands that had burncd deliciously against her skin when he'd swooped under her top. The heat at the pit of her stomach boiled at the memory. If he hadn't stopped, she'd have torn off her clothes ... and his.

Why the hell had he stopped? She bit her lower lip, revelling in how he'd taken over the kiss. Sweet mother of God, the kiss had been so hot, she should be a melted puddle at his feet. She frowned—what must he think of her for instigating a kiss with a man she barely knew? Would he shelve her behind the same unscrupulous partition as her father and twin?

What had she been thinking?
***

Rono kept pacing because it gave him an opportunity to control his anxiety. That kiss ... he'd had women throw themselves at him—her twin had thrown herself at him—but he'd always found it distasteful. A woman needed some form of decorum. A woman that threw herself at a man usually reminded him of his mother and her abandonment.

But that kiss.

He tried listening to his family head explain the process of the traditional marriage.The cavern of her mouth had been hot, smooth, and sweet. He'd tasted the juice she'd sipped and her own unique taste, one he was revving to sample again.

His eyes kept flicking to where she stood. She was frowning; what was she thinking? Would she change her mind? Was this too fast for her? He shook his head, recalling she'd agreed to do this, had not been forced.

She was sacrificing herself for her undeserving family, which was admirable in his point of view. Felicia wouldn't do it; the skinny twin was as self-serving as they came. His eyes flicked to Suto again, and he took in her rounded hips, the soft curve of her breasts. He recalled the soft smoothness of her skin under the blouse, and he had to look away and blink rapidly to tame his ardour.

Why wasn't he disgusted that she'd instigated the kiss? Why was he hoping for a repeat, perhaps with fewer clothes? The image of her spread naked before him on his bed made him stumble on his reply to his family head.

He cleared his throat and watched her move to reclaim her seat. She was uncomfortable; he noticed this, and shockingly, cared. What would Dave do to make her relax? He didn't want her feeling embarrassed or self-conscious. Like she'd blurted out earlier, they indeed had chemistry, a thing he'd never experienced with other women.

He'd erased marriage from his well-planned life, but with Suto, as his gaze steadied on her beautiful face, he realized he wanted her in his life. It explained why he'd accepted the idea of marriage without vehement refutes.

***

Suto's hands moved nervously as she fought with herself. Should she leave? What was the protocol for people who'd just agreed to get married for convenience?

She reached out for her drink in a bid to occupy her hands, but Rono appeared, swiping the drink away before she could pick it. She stared in amazement as he shook his head, still on the phone, and walked towards where she supposed was the kitchen.

She frowned. Was he back to being the inconsiderate gunman she'd met yesterday? She fumed. Dave had given her that drink; it was hers. Before she realized she was moving, she found herself at the kitchen staring at his broad back as he upturned the barely touched juice down the drain.

"Hey! That's mine." She frowned with her hands on her hips, resisting, with some difficulty, from tapping her sandaled foot like a disgruntled wife.

Rono turned startled eyes to her and immediately murmured an excuse, ending his call, his eyes never leaving hers, though narrowing in contemplation.

"Uh ..."

"I wasn't done with that." She sneered in challenge.

Suto really couldn't understand her need to fight him. She had a pressing urge to knock him off his high horse. Besides, it'd been rude to swipe the drink from her like that; he had to learn that she wasn't a cowering lady he could treat as less despite their predicament.

***

Rono's basic instinct was to retort with some choice, mean words. How dare she take that tone with him? His narrowed gaze made hardened men cower, but Suto glared back. So, he inhaled, tried channelling his cousin for a second, and realized his fault.

Fuck. Would he ever learn to be as charming as Dave? His aim had been to change her flat drink and get her a fresh one, but he'd obviously bumbled that, judging from her furious mien.

"I'm sorry," he began, and almost laughed at her confused expression. "I wanted to get you a fresh drink. I assumed that one would've been flat after being untouched for a while."

He kept his steady gaze on her.

"Oh." Her hands dropped from her curvy hips, and her expressive face held embarrassment. She bit her lower lip. "I didn't know ... shit ... I should go."

She swivelled so fast to march away, Rono was left dumbfounded.

He ran after her. "Hey, hold up a second."

He swooped in front of her, stopping her from getting her bag on the couch. He grabbed her shoulders and then dropped his hands because when she looked up at him, he had the pressing urge to drag her to him and squash his lips to hers.

He swallowed, blinking, "I've never been in a relationship ... I don't know how to ... shit ..."

His obvious nervousness seemed to make her feel better. Suto sighed and relaxed.

"Dinner?" he blurted. "We need to know ourselves, at least," he explained in a rush.

"Tomorrow." She nodded.

His throat clogged. He'd hoped for that evening. He sighed and nodded.

***

He didn't come the next day, or two days later, and the rest of the week passed without an appearance. Yet, he communicated with her father about marriage arrangements through calls.

Suto hated herself for caring—she shouldn't care, yet, she worried why he'd offered dinner. Had she been mistaken about the flash of disappointment in his eyes when she'd insisted the dinner be the next day? Was this payback for not following his plan? He had her number—if he was busy, he should've called. Or maybe, he hadn't saved it as she'd called him only that one time she'd visited his home.

She had considered calling him every time she'd come to the same conclusion that he might not have saved her number, but would always change her mind.

Her father knocked on her room door.

"I'm ready," she griped, wondering again what sort of dratted function he would insist she escort him to. If it was a legal event, she'd die of boredom.

When she stepped out of the room, dressed in a black flare dress with more make-up than she used on a normal day, the doorbell chimed.

"Suto, get the door!"

"I'm not the maid," she grumbled as she passed her father's closed room.

"I heard that," he snapped.

She hurried on medium, peep-toe heels to open the door without checking.

She got slammed with the sheer brilliance of Rono's handsomeness and stood staring speechless, shocked that he stood there after she'd fantasized about him every day since the last time she'd seen him.

"Suto, you look ... stunning." Rono's voice had gone husky at the sight of her.

"What are you doing here?" She walked out and stood with him on the veranda, not wanting her dad to hear them.

"I'm here for our dinner date."

He cleared his throat and looked away for a second as if to control himself.

Her eyes widened. "Over a week later?"

His smile was arrogant.

"Look who's counting. You missed me, babe?"

He smoothed a tendril of hair from her temple, the action startling both of them, but he maintained his smile.

Two reactions battled for supremacy in Suto: fury for his effrontery, and instant lust. She wanted to kiss him again at the unguarded act of tenderness. She was about to open her mouth to say something acerbic when the door behind her closed, and the key turned in the lock.

She swivelled in shock and knocked. "Daddy, I'm out here, and—"

"Go with the young man, Suto," he griped.

She leaned to the side, watching him through the window slides walking away, still in his pyjamas. How confusing, since she was supposed to escort ...

"Did you guys plan this?" Her heart tripped over the thought as she turned to find Rono's discomfort.

He shrugged.

"Surprise," he muttered, straightening his navy blue suit over a tie-less white shirt.

Suto scoffed and stared pointedly at him. "You could've called, you know."

"Didn't know what to say," he murmured, looking everywhere but at her.

"So, you had my number this whole time?"

"Saved it the first time you called."

Warmth bloomed in her stomach, spreading to her heart. How could he be an asshole and yet adorable at the same time?

"So, dinner?" he asked.

"I have no choice as my father has locked me out," she commented wryly, gushing with warmth when his hand grabbed her arm, helping her down the short steps. He didn't let go until she was seated at the back of his car.

The dinner at the private restaurant of the exclusive De-Castle Hotel became more than she'd expected after the first twenty minutes when he'd cleared his throat into their awkward silence, seeming to let go of his reservations to become a doting dinner date.

And by some silent agreement, they never mentioned what their marriage would or wouldn't entail. Instead, Rono seemed entirely interested in her career and impressed with her achievements in providing more than average healthcare services to the rural areas she'd been transferred to despite the holdups and speed-bumps of the bureaucratic system; a fit her family had always scoffed about.

Through the dinner, she sat on a cloud as she basked in his genuine interest and honesty as he answered questions about himself in detail. Though he seemed to avoid any questions that would lead to the issue demanding their marriage, she overlooked his not so subtle avoidance, believing he'd trust her more when they tied the knot.

She had thoroughly enjoyed herself and had been unwilling to let the night end when he escorted her to her door. An irrational fear of not seeing him again engulfed her heart.

"Should I expect you after another week?" She broke the tense silence while waiting for her father to get the door.

The arrogant smile appeared as she'd expected.

"Are you afraid I'll run, Princess?"

Was he a mind reader? She scoffed despite the joy of being called princess. "You've an inflated regard of yourself."

Chuckling, he chucked her endearingly before walking away as her father unlocked the door.

"Don't worry, the next time we dine, it'll be as a married couple."

CHAPTER SEVEN

Shelter Afrique

After his whirlwind marriage, Rono had ransacked his father's study for over a week, as opposed to honeymooning with his lovely wife.

Apart from her comment about their chemistry the first time they'd kissed and the conversations during their date, they'd not spoken about what their marriage would entail; there'd been no time with the convoluted marriage arrangements.

Consummating the marriage could complicate things. What if she got pregnant when it was time to divorce? Mistakes happened. His heart flipped as he imagined Suto pregnant and kids running around the house ... He wanted that, though he'd never believed it was possible for him.

His wife probably knew he'd killed; her father would've made sure. No woman wanted to remain in such a marriage. He'd not thought he'd ever marry, but now, he wanted to try. He wanted to be good for Suto. He couldn't explain it, but he wanted to convince her, and he'd planned to do that after the marriage ...

Except, an offhand comment from one of the chiefs during the marriage rites had sent him searching through his father's study, reading through documents and generally ignoring Suto and Dave.

When he'd read through his diary, he'd confirmed that his dad must have been suspecting the conspiracy to kill him. Rono had found several variables, but he still wasn't getting the full picture, so he'd called his private investigator.

Uncle Timothy, who'd been unable to hide his displeasure at his marriage, had called earlier to inform him of The Table's magnanimity to see him after he'd rudely refused their first summons. The lawyer had no say in his life, but he'd had no qualms scolding Rono for not seeking his advice before marrying, especially with everything happening. Timothy had not wished him a happy married life.

With over an hour before the meeting, Rono went to see his P.I. He'd deliberately fixed the meeting down the street from The Table's venue—Prestige Lounge.

He drove past the legal business which was a cover for The Table's narcotic deals; he'd just discovered his father owned seventy-five percent shares of Prestige Lounge, but his will had reflected only twenty-five percent, which meant his interest was way more than he'd been told.

Abel parked under the shade of trees in the fast-developing, high rise area. The driver left the car at the same moment the back door opened and the P.I. climbed in beside Rono.

"Marcus," he greeted.

"Mr. Ating." The small man sighed. "I've not been able to string my findings together. So many variables are hanging, though my gut says they're related."

Rono nodded, understanding what the man meant since he'd been experiencing the same thing.

"So, while I couldn't pin them, I decided to make a dossier on each of them, and found out that they, excluding your father, were in alternate deals with another big dealer. All efforts to find out proved abortive; I believe this big player might be the key to unravel everything."

With a grunt, Rono collected the file and looked through.

"You did well. I'll study this later, but, could you look into Timothy Owoyem for me?"

"Your father's attorney?"

"For this investigation, treat him like this." He raised the file.

"Of course."

"Funds will drop by this evening," he assured and shook hands with the P.I. before he stepped out of the car.

***

Rono marched into Prestige Lounge thirty minutes before the agreed time. He sauntered in as though he owned the place, which, literally, he did.

The cool and dark exterior proved welcoming after the harsh sun outside. He got to the mahogany wood of the bar and slapped a golden card on the counter, cutting off the barman's polite tell-off.

The man stood straighter at seeing the card—his father's pass into the inner rooms, which Rono had found in his diary as though it'd been there waiting for him.

Rono followed the employee down the corridor, the beautiful rug muting their steps as they approached closed double doors with sounds of levity beyond them.

When the man reached out to knock, Rono stopped him and sent him away. He took deep breaths knowing these men weren't expecting him yet.

He pulled open the doors and stood there until they noticed him.

"Gentlemen," he said, and walked towards the head of the long, polished table where Umeh sat, filling his dad's seat with his bulk.

"My seat, sir," he said calmly.

"What insult!" Tony sputtered for his father's sake, rising to his feet and opening his mouth—

Obviously to say something, but that was the only thing he got out because Rono, without looking away from Umeh, grabbed Tony's neck and squeezed.

"My. Seat. Sir."

With the sound of Tony's choking echoing in the room, Umeh stumbled out of the president's seat, his cigar a forgotten spectre on the marble floor.

Rono dropped Tony into his chair, elegantly slid to stand before his father's seat, and stared at the men on The Table. Pinning eleven of them with his fury, he arranged his suit and sat, crossing a leg.

"I am here."

Silence and tension thickened the air.

"Find a space, man." He frowned at Umeh, who bristled but walked with all the dignity he could muster to the table and tapped another member, who scooted over for him so he could still sit at the head.

This way, Rono had both Umehs, on his right and left.

More silence ... and then, someone cleared his throat.

"Son, this isn't how things are done. I know you haven't met me, but—"

"Mbon Ubon," he began, then turned to Umeh. "Anthony Umeh Senior and Junior."

He pointed at everyone and mentioned names.

Silence again

Tony scoffed. "So, you know our names. Big deal."

Rono looked at him. "You mustn't be really smart."

"Obviously, your father spoke about us—"

"No, he didn't."

Rono leaned back with his right elbow bent and his hand supporting his jaw.

"Since no one is talking, I will." He was so calm, it was like ice flowed in his veins. "I didn't come here to claim my father's seat. Before his murder, I knew he wanted out. I understand there's a process to this and a price, and I understand his interest is enough for the price and to spare.

"You, as colleagues of my dad, will sort out the price, and in your magnanimity, will deposit the spare in his account by Friday.

"Let me warn, I am not my father. I am not nice or forgiving." His eyes narrowed evilly. "I will find my father's killers. I pray none of you are among."

He then got to his feet, straightened his suit, and sauntered towards the door. "Enjoy your Sunday, gentlemen."

CHAPTER EIGHT

Jacob Ating's Mansion

They'd kissed without knowing their names.

The memory made her warm all over whenever she relished it, which amounted to always. She'd gotten to know his full name, Borono-Abasi, a lovely name meaning *answer to God*, but she loved that Dave called him Ron, and others, Rono.

She'd not yet decided what she'd call him because she'd not gotten the chance to. After their marriage, over a week ago, she'd seen him only in passing, most times when he was leaving the house. It didn't feel like marriage to her, even one of convenience—it felt like she'd just changed residence. She'd expected more, especially, after their one-time dinner.

It'd been news to her that he was a prince, and she'd confirmed it when the elders and chiefs of his family had come in royal regalia to perform the traditional marriage rites. It'd been the first and only time she'd seen her husband in anything other than a suit.

He'd looked so uncomfortable in the gold brocade jumper over a beaded wrapper, shoes, and cap, and she'd giggled. If someone had told her Rono slept in a suit, she'd totally believe them. The princely garb looked fine on him, though.

She'd taken a snapshot of his face when he'd frowned at a chief from his family who wouldn't stop talking, thereby stalling the event. It'd been no surprise when Dave had approached the chief, spoken in his ear, and the event had moved swiftly after that.

Suto shook her head. Those two were like two sides of the same coin, different, but the same. Sometimes, she felt they had the same thought process. Though Dave was lighter and understood consideration, his cousin was just a big block of man force ... sexy man force, and, surprisingly, devoted to God.

He'd insisted they do everything the Reverend Father asked, from the few days of compulsory marriage counselling to full-body medical tests, even the Sunday Thanksgiving.

After the celebrations the previous day, she'd have preferred sleep, but had had to sit through the Mass, feeling like she'd drop any minute. Rono had kept giving her concerned glances and had felt her neck at some point, as if wondering if she were ill. The action had melted her heart, though considering his ignoring her now, it might've been cursory.

They'd dressed in traditional garb for the event; she in white lace blouse over purple wrapper and gele while he'd worn the same white lace in jumper, with purple embroideries and a cap he'd pulled off for church's sake. She had thought they'd worn colours pertaining to their lives, purple for royalty and white for her profession.

She'd been given a room which she'd felt was theirs, but when he'd not shown up that night after their chapel wedding, she'd learnt the next day that his room was down the hall. She'd wondered what the kiss had been for, but recalled that she'd instigated that kiss. Obviously, he didn't want intimacy with her—she was not his type, perhaps; sexy guys loved girls as thin as her sister.

Suto had experienced that sort of rejection several times. She should've been used to it, but it still hurt. Her sister had been the first to be with him. They must have been intimate in that time, and she worried she'd not compare.

Everything was so messed up. Maybe, him not being sexually attracted to her was a good thing. It'd be weird to have slept with twin sisters.

"Is it the TV or me?" Dave broke into her tumultuous thoughts.

"What?" She turned to him with startled eyes.

"Your frown, it's bothersome. Is your room okay, are you comfortable?"

Her room was fit for royalty. She smiled—on second thought, she herself was royalty now. "Dave, you've been the nicest. Thanks for making me comfortable."

Her gratitude was genuine.

Dave sighed. "Be patient with him. He's dealing with serious stuff right now."

She nodded and stared at the movie for a moment.

"Can we do pizza for dinner?" She wriggled her brows at him, and he laughed.

"Anything for you, sweetie."

Why couldn't Rono be more like Dave?

"I'm going out for a bit. I'll be back with the pizza. You'll be okay for a few hours, right?"

The clock displayed one-thirty p.m. "Yes."

"Be back soon." He grabbed his keys. "Lock the door."

Suto nodded and did as told.

Thirty minutes later, she was ready to scratch her eyes out from boredom. As an obstetrician and gynaecologist with experience in general surgery, she was used to being busy. Her application at the Teaching Hospital to be redeployed out of the metropolis remained under consideration, and since she was on leave, she couldn't do anything about it.

Sighing, she flipped through channels until she found MTV and laughed her head off as she tried to learn the shoki dance—how ridiculous to squat with open arms and going up as though lifting something and then dumping the imaginary thing, all done in tandem with the music.

She was taking a break when her phone rang.

"Justin!"

"Babes, what's up? You busy?"

"Nah, what do you need?"

"I have a fibroid surgery at my PP for two-thirty p.m. Can you make it?"

"Err ..." Could she? With so much to consider, she wished Dave was here to ask. She shrugged—not like Rono would notice her absence.

"Please, say yes. You're my calming balm, you know, and I appreciate your brilliance."

"Okay, okay, flattery will get you places. I'll be there."

He chuckled. "Expecting you. Same account number?"

"Yep. See you soon."

Feeling lighter, she rushed upstairs to grab her knapsack of supplies. She always had some stuff for emergencies and times when the hospital supplies took too long to arrive. She had a dealer who supplied it at minimum price. Justin's private clinic must have updated medical supplies, but she just always felt comfortable going with hers, which made her feel ready for emergencies.

***

"Where the hell have you been?"

His anger was like hot wind. Suto reared back and raised her eyebrows at him and Dave standing behind him. The surgery had taken longer than expected, and she'd had to make a report of her observations during the operation and treatment suggestions before leaving. It was only eight p.m., so he had no right to bark at her.

Dave's apologetic expression made her swallow her retort and reply calmly. "I had an impromptu surgery."

She raised the lab-coat draped on her arm while adjusting the knapsack on her right shoulder.

***

Rono could feel the fury building like a volcano in his chest at her casual reply. When he'd returned and found the house empty as opposed to Dave's report that she was home alone and he should talk with her, he'd been scared out of his mind. Didn't she realize how dangerous it was for her as his wife?

"I don't care!"

"Ron—"

"Do you know how lethal it is for you now that you bear my name?"

He knew he should calm down. He knew his reaction was wrong, but he couldn't stop himself. The fear for her safety made him mad.

She didn't retreat as he towered over her, glowering.

"I don't, because you failed to tell me." She made fists as if to control her anger and refused to look at Dave, who appeared torn between them.

"It's common sense, Suto—"

"Ron!" Dave looked aghast.

She breathed harshly through her nose. "It's common sense that you communicate what's expected of your wife to her, if not before the wedding, then immediately after it! But no, you were too busy playing avenger."

Rono scoffed. "Look who's playing the slighted wife."

His mouth twisted in disdain.

"Christ, Ron, stop."

Suto narrowed her eyes at him, and she seemed incensed. When her left palm flew to slap him, her lab-coat dropped from her arm, and the phone in the pocket made a sharp sound as it hit the floor. Before any of them could reckon that, he blocked the slap.

"So predictable. Don't ever try this—"

She knocked off his words when her knee slammed into his groin. Anger radiated from her as she stood there. While he was bent over, she slammed her elbow on the back of his head, the force propelling his head into the back of the sofa. Then, he fell on his back, his hands still over his groin as he groaned.

"Wow," Dave breathed.

"Now, never, ever speak to me in that tone again. I might be married to you, but I'm my own woman. And if my father wasn't an idiot, we'd never have met." She kicked his shin before grabbing her coat and bag and taking the stairs two at a time.

"I am so proud right now." Dave grinned, staring down at his groaning cousin.

"Whose side are you on?" he grunted and struggled to his knees.

"You're asking?" Dave seemed shocked. "Her side, of course. God knew not to give you a timid woman. She go show you pepper," he concluded in pidgin.

"Asshole."

"Look in the mirror, man. Better go apologise to her, and when you're done, microwave the pizza, feed her, and level up with her. Do you understand?"

Rono adjusted his aching balls.

"Yes, daddy." He sneered with his hands on his hips, breathing through the receding pain.

Dave chuckled as he walked towards the front door. "Lock up."

Rono weighed the distance to lock up and the stairs—he took the stairs. He had scores to settle with his wife. Weird how he'd found her anger sexy.

He knocked and tried her door, finding it locked.

"Open the door, Suto!"

"Fuck off!"

"This is my house. You cannot lock me out," he snapped.

"It's your father's house."

He smiled. "Same difference."

He snatched his gun and silencer. Affixing both, he stood to the side and pointed at the lock. Two muffled pops later, he was inside her room where she'd been undressing. She had on a T-shirt over lace panties.

"What the fuck? I could've been standing in harm's way."

"But you weren't." He prowled towards her.

"Stay right there!" she commanded, raising her fists in a fight stance.

He raised his eyebrows with a smile, his heart twisting at how beautiful she looked.

"You want to fight, uh?" He dropped his gun on a counter, shrugged off his suit, and unbuttoned his cuffs and shirt after pulling it from his trousers.

"What are you doing?" Her voice didn't sound so sure, her arms lowering while she stared at him bared before her.

"Preparing to fight." He slid off his shoe, socks, and then his trousers.

Suto gasped.

"But ..." She seemed to swallow hard. "But you don't need to pull off your trousers," she complained while her eyes got stuck on his grey boxers which he knew sculpted his physique so well, it left nothing to the imagination. She suddenly grew speechless.

"I want to be as comfortable as you." He nodded at her panties and took a fight stance, then without warning, he jump-kicked her wrist, and before she could recover, he had her pinned on the wall beside her window, shoving his thigh in between hers to avoid her groin kick.

His hand loosely rounded over her throat. "Where did you learn to fight?"

His eyes devoured her beautiful face.

"Justin taught me at medical school."

Her eyes bored into his as he pressed his hardness against her core.

"Who the fuck is Justin?" he growled, surprised to be jealous of an unknown man.

"My friend and—"

"I'm going to kill him," he declared.

"Uh?"

With her mouth open in shock, he swooped down and claimed her lips.

It was like the first kiss but more. The instant warmth between them simmered and boiled into heat. His hand slipped from her throat, caressing a path down to her heaving breasts. He grabbed one heavy globe while his tongue plundered her mouth.

Suto must be able to feel the solid length of his hard heat pressed against her core, and she rubbed against it, searching for more friction. Noticing her efforts, he bent his knee and ground into her, enjoying her gasp of pleasure and the tightening of her arms around his neck.

He continued this and enjoyed watching her deepening frown as she chased the end this sort of pleasure usually brought. Rono thought he'd blow his load prematurely like a teenage boy when she moaned, quickened her movements, and soaked her panties, which meant his boxers were soaked, too.

She was still heaving when he pulled away and slid his hand into her undies, finding her dripping cleft and sliding in. Curving his finger upward, he knew he'd found her spot when she moaned long while standing on her toes as though to get his fingers deeper.

"Fuck, you're so beautiful." He stared at her as his fingers curved in more, his thumb tweaking her clit. "I can't wait to feel your heat surround me ..."

"Then do it now!" she gasped, shifting from his fingers and pulling off her shirt.

While she hurriedly unclasped her bra, Rono pulled of his singlet.

"You're too sexy," she accused and wriggled off her panties.

He chuckled, then groaned when he saw her big boobs and the dark patch at her apex. He rushed off his boxers, and it was her turn to groan when his appendage swung hard and proud, its big, mushroom head bobbing and leaking pre-cum.

Suto licked her lips and went on her knees before him.

"No ... please, I'll ..."

She licked the head.

"Just a taste," she murmured, her eyes glazed as she petted his dick, licking from the base to the head before swallowing him.

Rono grunted and groaned, his hips moving without conscious thought. The pleasure proved mind-blowing, and he was close to exploding, so he forcefully pulled her from his dick ...

"Next time," he gasped and helped her onto the king-size bed.

Suto seemed to pull into herself as he began kissing her soft belly.

"Please ignore the extra flesh," she blurted.

He stopped his exploration, crawled up to face her, and frowned. "You were a confident, damn sexy woman a moment ago. Where did that come from?"

She averted her gaze and turned her face away from him.

"Look at me," he growled, and her eyes returned to his.

"I ..." She cleared her throat. "You've been with my twin, and I'm nothing like her."

Her eyes lowered.

Shock must have registered on his face, and he hoped she'd seen it.

"I've never been with your sister! I couldn't even stand the sight of her. I hated her more because she couldn't take the hint or ... stop being a damn pest!"

"You've never slept with her?"

He could hear the awe and even the hope in her voice despite him having spoken ill of her twin.

"That's the only thing you heard?" He nuzzled her neck, and he was sure his heart would leak from his pores as it melted from her giggles. "Where's your tattoo?"

She gasped. "How did you know that?"

"First day in your garden," he murmured distractedly as he tasted her neck.

"It was temporary."

Now that it wasn't there, he kind of missed it. "It was beautiful."

He lowered his body onto hers, perfectly aligning his hardness against her wetness. He moaned and flexed his hips while kissing his way up 'til he melded with her lips.

The kiss got heated again in seconds. It was as though his soul accepted hers and hers accepted his. They were perfect together. At the heavy warmth in his chest, his lips itched to profess undying love, but he feared she'd not believe him ... It was too soon.

So he settled for something else.

"You're the sexiest, most beautiful woman I've ever met. I never fancied chubby ladies, but you ... You make a mockery of all I've known. I've never felt this ... connected to any woman like I do with you," he whispered.

Suto blinked away the tears. Even Rono couldn't quite believe it. This was magical, like two souls finding their way home. The shock of his own words still coursed through him, but he focused on her gaze which mirrored his emotions.

"Let's be more connected then," she whispered coyly and widened her legs.

"You naughty minx," he groaned, rushed to his knees, and was about to slide his dick into her when he took a moment to admire her core.

He leaned on his haunches, grabbed himself, and stroked the long, hard length while his left hand found her clit and rubbed.

She exploded with one touch. And while she was still riding the climax, he plunged into her, sighing as her wetness clutched him.

He straightened, raised her thigh, and rotated his hips, which made her scream her pleasure. He had found her spot, so he concentrated on pounding it and was rewarded with multiple gushes as she climaxed.

"Should I stop?"

She was whimpering, but she immediately shook her head. He grinned and leaned down to suck a brown nipple into his mouth.

He let go of her leg while still joined with her and grabbed her breasts, settling in to suckle one after the other, his eyes shut as he pulled her nipple deep. Suto came again.

"Fuck, I didn't even move." He got to his knees and began pounding her. "I won't last, baby," he sobbed.

His hips quickened, slamming harder, the rhythmic sound of skin against skin echoing in the room. Her response to him blew his mind.

"Next time, I want from the back," he declared.

"Yes, please."

She nodded, and that pushed him off the edge. Groaning and grunting, he shivered, flexing his hips through his climax. She joined him once again on the crest of this wave and fell with a whimpering moan.

"When are we doing the back?" she asked a few moments later.

Rono's chuckle was muffled by her shoulder. His body shook above hers.

"Let me catch my breath, dear." He raised himself and smiled at her. "And I'll tap that ass."

***

He had her pinned against the head-board, her ass slightly out as he pounded into her, grabbing her luscious buttocks and spreading it, probably to watch his dark length slide in and out, bordered by her fair butt-cheeks. His dick must now be coated with her cream and her ass red from his spanking. The climax came on more intense than the first.

"I can't get enough of you," he said as they lay together. Then, he jumped out of her embrace and sat up. "Shit!"

"What?" Alarm coursed through her.

"I forgot to feed you."

"Uh?"

"Dave asked me to microwave the pizza, feed you, and then talk to you after the apology."

Suto frowned. "So this was just an apology?"

"That would mean it won't happen again, and that's a lie. This is happening a lot." His face was goofy when he leaned in to kiss her. "Let me get the pizza."

She moaned in protest.

"Another?"

He widened his eyes, and she nodded shyly.

"God, you'll be the death of me ... and I love it," he murmured before kissing her. "Be right back, babe. Besides, we need to talk."

She blew him kisses while he pulled on his pants because he couldn't locate his boxers. Then, grinning, he went downstairs.

Suto crawled out of bed to ease her bladder. When she returned, she picked up his suit from the floor. His knife pouch fell out, bringing a smile to her face as she recalled the first time she'd seen them.

Laying the pouch on the counter, she pulled out four, stainless steel knives and mimed throwing them …

That's when she heard it.

Pots clattered, leading her to chuckle, believing Rono didn't know his way around the kitchen. But then, she heard glass break and became worried.

"Is everything okay?" She stepped out of the room and was shocked to find a masked man on the landing.

"Run, Suto!" Rono screamed from downstairs.

She stood there, numb to her bones and unable to move. She'd forgotten she was naked until the masked man pulled his mask and whistled, his eyes raking her form.

Her breath came in pants, terror clogging her throat. She reached down to cover herself and discovered the knives in her hands. She looked up at the same moment the killer saw her weapons.

She flung it without aiming, shocked to hear his grunt of pain just before his gun went off, the bullet hitting the wall away from where she stood.

She ducked, raced into the room, and snatched more knives with shaky hands, having heard his heavy tread as he approached while sounds of struggle filtered up the stairs.

She'd been pointing the knife at the door, wondering if she'd be lucky this time, when her eyes fell on the gun. Her hands shook as she aimed at the door, and as the attacker appeared, she squeezed the trigger. Just a muffled pop, the gun jerked in her hands, and she stared in consternation as he staggered and fell.

It felt surreal, the realization that she'd killed someone making her shake all over, the beginning of a monstrous melt down, but then, a gun shot went off downstairs.

"Ron!" she whimpered, racing down the corridor, the weapon heavy in her hand.

"Well, well …" another killer said when she appeared on the landing of the stairs.

Her nakedness distracted him. She just aimed and shot; he dropped with a thud.

God, how many were they? *Please be okay*, she prayed.

"Suto …" The sound came from the kitchen.

She lost all caution and raced down the stairs, across the dining and into the kitchen.

It lay in disarray. Blood smeared a path from the gas-cooker to behind the counter. She followed it, tears streaming down her face, her hands shaking as she pointed the gun.

Sobs exploded at seeing Rono bleeding from a bullet wound and a few cuts. She slammed to her knees and gathered him into her arms. Her medical training seemed to have melted from her brain—she suddenly didn't know what to do for him but cry.

"Ssh." He patted her arm with bloodied hands from holding his rib. "I'm okay, baby …"

"He's not. He's going to die." A stout man, dressed like his dead comrades, suddenly stood before them.

Suto searched for the gun and found it at the killer's feet, where she'd dropped it in her concern for her husband. She sobbed, pulling a weak Rono to herself.

"Leave us alone," she wailed, tears and mucus drenching her face.

"You killed my men." The stout man didn't sound distraught at his loss. "Dead men don't tell tales. Thank you. It adds to the juiciness of tomorrow's breaking news, when Borono Ating is discovered to have murdered his father to inherit some paltry sum just to upgrade his drug business. Those two would pass as partners he'd double-crossed, and then, I will be able to deal in—"

"Honey, are you done?" a woman called out and walked into the kitchen.

"You should've stayed in the car," he groaned.

"It wasn't exciting." She stared at Suto and grimaced. "Were you his whore?"

"You're the look out," the man grunted.

"Isabella is looking out." She straightened her black T-shirt and looked round the kitchen as though she was on tour. "This is a nice kitchen."

"Stella, please return to the car."

"I'm not leaving until you kill her, so you'll stop staring at her huge … breasts." She sneered the last word.

Suto whimpered, the surreal feeling increasing as she listened to the insane couple while Rono became weaker in her arms. Her medical instincts had returned, but she was faced with these people who would let her husband die in her arms.

Tears gushed down her face. She had just met him. She was pretty sure she loved him, and she regretted not telling him earlier. Sniffling, she leaned down and kissed his jaw while the mad couple bickered.

"I love you, Ron. I love you so much. I love you," she whispered through a clogged throat, sobbing on his shoulder.

"Daddy!"

Suto looked up and found a teenage girl rushing to the mad couple. Were they like a family of killers?

"Why are you not in the car?" the man barked.

"I—"

"That will be because of me, Okoko."

Suto recognized the new man, and hope flared in her heart.

"Uncle Timothy," she whispered in elation.

"Err …" The man looked confused.

"Honey, what do we do?" his wife jittered, holding on to their daughter.

"I suggest you drop your weapons and get on your knees," Timothy said.

The woman and child complied.

"I can explain …" Okoko dropped the rod he'd been holding, and right before their eyes, his face transformed to that of a benign man.

"You killed Jacob and tried to ..." Timothy looked at Suto and Rono in the corner. "Can you save him?" he asked soberly.

She nodded, gently laying Rono on the floor, and then raced out of the kitchen, not caring about her nakedness. She returned wearing her T-shirt with her knapsack already opened.

Rono was alive because the bullet had lodged inches above his heart—she needed to get him to a hospital. Her hands shook as she tried to staunch the heavy blood flow. She couldn't know how bad the stab wounds were—she needed an X-ray, but she managed the bleeding as best she could while whispering to a barely conscious Rono.

"Detectives." Timothy ushered in two plain clothes cop and five uniformed policemen.

While they cuffed the deadly family, she directed how Rono should be gently lifted to a car.

Timothy got in and pulled out while she dialled her friend's number.

"Justin, please ..." She choked on her tears while cradling Rono's head on her lap.

"My God, Suto, what—"

"I'm bringing my husband to the clinic."

CHAPTER NINE

Genesis Clinic

"I've never seen anything like it."

It was almost two weeks after the incident, and Suto was going crazy trying to find out why Rono was still only semi-conscious. She stared at him on the hospital bed, looking sleepy but generally unresponsive when spoken to.

"He lost a lot of blood, Suto," Justin pointed out.

"That was replaced."

"His body had gone into hypovolemic shock, and your timely treatment saved his life."

"You did say this isn't a coma."

"Suto, you know this isn't a coma, but I researched his symptoms."

Her eyes widened in hope.

"Though not usual, he's exhibiting a psychological response to the major trauma he's experienced. It's called a Stupor, where he's not unconscious, but isn't active, either."

"I've heard of that, but not how to bring him out of it, and it doesn't last this long."

Justin sighed. "The way you spoke about him, I believe he's a strong guy, a fighter. I need you to trust that he'll break out of this."

She nodded. "At least, I'm glad for his healing wounds and stable vitals."

"Exactly. He'll be fine."

He dragged her into a hug that lasted a while.

She needed the comfort and the boost in believing that Rono would be fine.

***

It was that stupid doctor overly hugging his wife that broke his numbness. Then, there was also his idiot cousin who felt he could touch his Suto whenever he pleased.

He wasn't allowing that.

Rono had been fighting a psychological battle. He recalled his terror when the first stab had pierced his rib because he'd turned with a smile, assuming Suto had entered the kitchen. If the stab had been at his back as planned, there was no way it would've missed a major organ.

He recalled reacting, lifting the first thing his hand touched, a pot, and smashing it on the intruder's head. He vaguely heard a command for someone to go upstairs. He blocked other stab attempts, taking two in his arm and one in his thigh when he screamed for Suto to run.

Then, Okoko had appeared, handing the attacker a gun which he instantly shot. They must have thought him dead, because Okoko had left the kitchen. All he could think about was Suto. He'd wanted to get to his feet and protect her; he'd wanted to tell her he loved her. And then, he'd seen her naked and had assumed the worse—had they raped her?

She'd been crying, and he'd tried to comfort her but had been too weak. He must have passed out because when he'd awoken, he'd been in the hospital, recovering.

How did that happen?

Numbness stole over his mind.

How had he survived that lethal experience? After all he'd done—granted, he'd been killing bad people, but it was still a sin, which was why he'd always gone for confessions, though guilt persisted.

It was unbelievable that he'd had a second chance, and from what the doctor said, it was because of the timely management of his wounds by his Suto. Only God had brought her to him. Though their meeting had come about in a bad situation, she'd brought light into his life and love into his heart.

He'd been battling with the guilt of not just being alive, but soiling Suto's light with his darkness, wondering if he could give her a divorce, but hurting when he imagined his life without her.

Then, the hugs had begun, and he'd realized that if he lost the will to live or let go of God's gift, someone else would take it. So, he'd decided to relinquish the guilt and accept God's grace.

"Is that Justin?" he croaked and watched as Suto almost fell in her haste to get to his bedside, crying and laughing at the same time.

"Yes, yes, it's Justin."

"I'm going to kill him for touching you," he growled, frowning at the shocked doctor.

Suto laughed, kissing his face all over. "You're fine … He's fine. Oh, Justin, don't look so scared. He's joking."

"No, I'm not." He eyed Justin while accepting Suto's hugs.

"Baby, Justin is married, has always been even when he taught me fight moves in medical school. We had this conversation just before …"

Justin nodded and proceeded to run check-ups certifying him okay.

* * *

"I don't know if it was midlife crisis, but Jacob just decided he wanted off The Table and decided he really wanted to pursue the crown."

Suto sat with Rono on the hospital bed while Dave and Timothy sat in the available chairs. Okoko was in custody, The Table had been exposed, arrests had been made, and Felicia was back home, but Rono wanted to know why everything had happened.

"He was listening to me." He sighed.

Suto kissed his hand joined with hers. "It wasn't your fault."

"Exactly," Dave grunted, nodding at Suto for saying the right thing.

Rono sighed. He knew they were right, but he felt responsible. His father had never wanted him in the business, and Dave had only been in it because he'd wanted to.

He'd carved a niche for himself, creating a company that dealt in granites and gravels for building and making roads. Then, he'd expanded it to cement and fuel haulage; he'd made so much money without the risks of the drug trade.

Granted, it had been funds from the drug trade that had helped him start big and grow bigger, but seeing the profitability, he'd wanted to help his father avoid the scandal of arrests, especially when the NDLEA became more conscientious in apprehending drug lords.

"It appears Okoko had found a new strain of marijuana that was selling out fast and channels to push it which would guarantee great profits that would not be shared on The Table.

"Your dad liked the idea. Okoko rushed into the deal with the trust that your dad would support when it mattered, but then, Jacob changed his mind, and the deal crumbled. He lost his money."

Rono nodded, recalling Okoko had told him he'd wanted out of The Table and that his dad had helped him. The man had lied the whole time, playing the string master and manipulating all situations.

"But you showed me a wrong will."

"It wasn't wrong, having calculated what he was willing to pay to leave The Table; that was his exact stake. He'd even planned to sell Prestige Lounge to any of the men, but Okoko had already infiltrated their minds ..."

"He was the alternate dealer The Table was transacting with," Rono said in realization, recalling what his P.I. had found out.

"And they were side-lining Jacob at this point, though they needed his money to complete the massive deal."

"But then, he was leaving The Table, taking the other side of his money away," Dave added.

They were getting the clear picture now.

"The money which he was going to get from the auction of his cache at Eastern Obolo." He shared a glance with Dave, and Dave shrugged at Suto who just shook her head with a smile.

"Exactly, but your father, in his usual magnanimity, had told Okoko about his cache, the deal, and the amount he would gift him as compensation for his losses, seeing as it was his fault."

"But one of the boys at Eastern Obolo said it was a lawyer. No offence, Suto, but I strongly believed it was your dad."

"None taken. I'd think the same thing, too, in the situation, especially after the stunt he'd pulled with my twin."

"That was Okoko covering his tracks and trying to set me up. But when he hadn't heard from his people, and you visited him talking about your girlfriend instead of your father's death, he switched and began manipulating you."

"He was the reason they'd not summoned you earlier. He'd been responsible in encouraging Umeh to bring his son while feeding him with dribble about how Jacob demeaned Tony, always comparing him to you, and that made Umeh antagonistic towards your father and unreasonably harsh towards your summons and the stipulations that would be given, which involved getting married."

"But you weren't happy I was getting married." Rono frowned.

"I wasn't happy about *who* you were getting married to, no offense, dear," he apologised to Suto.

She smiled. "None taken."

"I had discovered Ekwere's connections with Umeh and feared he would throw you under the bus to save himself."

"He'd done that already, except the cops had no evidence, and my sister has a history of going off to party for days while others worried for her safety." Suto huffed, pissed at her family.

"Don't be angry, babe. I'm glad it happened. It led me to you." His eyes bore into hers, and ...

"Okay, stop, we are right here," Dave protested while Timothy laughed.

The lovebirds smiled, shifting closer.

"So, who got the wine to Uncle Jacob?" Dave asked, sobering the light mood.

Timothy shook his head. "Okoko confessed that his wife spiked his food when he'd visited to share the news about the deal, and when Jacob slept, he'd injected him with a slow-killing poisonous drug. It wasn't the wine, and everybody on The Table was in on it. He confessed Oscar procured the poison."

Rono felt pissed. "That asshole manipulated me the whole time."

He recalled letting his guard down because of the domesticity they'd displayed, obviously staged.

"The case is closed. Suto is free. By the way, both dead guys were Sly and Jo."

Rono and Dave shared a startled glance—they had to look into X-raying their employees to expose other moles.

"Though it was self-defence, it was simpler to pin their deaths on Okoko as part of covering his tracks."

"Oh, thank God." Suto slumped on Rono's good shoulder, and he laid his head on hers.

"He was there that night with his family because, after killing you, they were leaving town. The judge might give the kid juvenile detention, depending on her age and extent of involvement, but her parents are going to jail.

"I'm sorry, Borono," Timothy apologized when he saw his sadness. "The idea was to kill Jacob, get his stake for the deal because Okoko had assured them you wouldn't be interested due to things your father had spoken about you. They never envisaged you'd investigate and avenge."

Dave chuckled while Suto kissed his stubble and grinned. "My own personal avenger."

CHAPTER TEN

Rono's Home

Suto loosened the blind-fold from Rono's eyes and watched the grin on his face as he viewed his furnished apartment for the first time, two weeks after he'd regained consciousness. Dave had really out-done himself.

"Man, you're the best." He hugged his cousin, both of them patting backs as only men do. "So, where's the second surprise?"

He looked around.

"Uh?" Dave frowned.

And then, Suto slid into Rono's arms, circled his neck, and spoke into his ear. "I hope we have a daughter, and I hope she has your lips and eyes."

He stepped back in shock. His eyes swivelled to her stomach and back to her eyes.

"That one time?" he whispered.

Suto rolled her eyes. "It was twice, though that doesn't matter because one time is enough."

"What are you guys talking about?" Dave looked from one to the other.

Rono turned stunned eyes to him. "You're going to be an uncle."

"Uh?" After a second, he rushed Suto, lifting her off her feet and twirling her.

"Dave, be careful!" Rono growled, snatching her from his arms and hugging her protectively.

"You know that could've been my kid, right? I saw her first."

Rono's frown was instant and thunderous.

Suto giggled, and Dave grinned, slapping his cousin on the shoulder.

"Calm down, you too dey vibrate," he joked in pidgin.

***

He sighed and visibly calmed down. His reaction melted her heart. When he looked at her, his brown eyes shone with love.

"Have I told you how much I love you?"

"Oh, God, not again," Dave grumbled, walking away. "I'll be in the kitchen."

Suto chuckled. "Not today."

"I love you, Suto. I've always craved a real family, but never allowed myself to believe it would happen. At first, women were just annoying, and then, I did bad stuff to avenge my dad. I believed I was a write off for redemption.

"But then, you came along and changed everything. You saved my heart, my life, and now, you're giving me my deepest desire, a family ... a home. I don't even know where to start being grateful ... what should I do, Suto ... what do you desire?"

She lifted her face and melded her lips to his, kissing him so deeply, her toes tingled and his groin hardened against her stomach.

"We'll be grateful to God for bringing us together, and all I want from you is your brand of love." She rubbed her nose with his.

"I hope our daughter is chubby like you."

"She better be." She huffed, and they both laughed. "But a son must be like you, hard and sexy."

"Speaking of hard ..." He dragged her close, his hand lowering to grab her butt, which he squeezed and then pressed her to him. "Care to find out what that is?"

He flexed his erection against her.

Suto swallowed, her eye glazing over with desire. "I've been waiting all that time at the clinic, so ... yes. I don't just want to find out. I want to play with it. Besides, you owe me a lick."

She eyed him, biting her lower lip, and he groaned, probably recalling their only night together.

"Where's our room?" he called out to Dave.

"It's the middle of the afternoon, guys," Dave protested.

"Follow me." She winked and raced towards the rooms.

Rono gave chase, grinning when she giggled.

Dave smiled when he heard their room door slam. Rono deserved this happiness and a family. He'd been guilty for his aunt's sake and had stuck close, making sure he was nothing like his father or his aunt, Rono's mom.

Sighing, he popped a piece of meat from the small chops prepared for Rono's homecoming, relishing the burst of flavours. The lovebirds would eat later.

He hoped Rono would be sexually satisfied enough not to be furious when he discovered he'd put up his father's house for sale. He filled his plate with puff-puff, spring-rolls, samosas, and fried meat, and proceeded to the sitting room to wait. He turned on the TV and murmured, "Home sweet home."

THE END

ABOUT THE AUTHOR

Emem Bassey loves romance in all its forms, especially blended with action, adventure/magic, definitely with a plus size heroine. She discovered the joys of writing at age 17 and hasn't stopped since. She staunchly believes the world is filled with tragedy, so she writes to entertain and lighten the heart.

Emem lives at Uyo, Akwa Ibom State, Nigeria and is basically a ghost to her neighbours. Connect with her on Instagram: https://www.instagram.com/flare2blaze/

The Messenger
JULIE ONOH

THE MESSENGER by Julie Onoh

Innocent Odion has never fully understood the meaning of the word ''Upside-Down'' until her simple life takes a dark tumble into the gangster underworld.

Now her innocence is wielded as a dangerous weapon in a world of masterful cunning.

In a dangerous race against time, the hunted becomes the hunter. She must fight for her family and for love.

CHAPTER ONE

Odion Osahon

"O wa ooo!"

No response came from the bus conductor.

"Conductor, O wa! I'm stopping here." She stretched from her seat to tap the man's shoulder and repeated, "Conductor."

The man turned back, the crooked scar across his left eyebrow deepening his scowl into a menacing horror. "My friend, sit down before I break your neck. No vex me ooo."

Odion Osahon drew back, trembling. She was done for. This must be a one-chance vehicle; the one operated by robbers or kidnappers who posed as commercial drivers to nab unsuspecting victims in one chance.

Would they drive her to an unknown destination? Would they just rob or also kill her? She swallowed. The police force didn't seem capable of curbing this cancerous threat, and the people of the land had simply learnt to accept this ill trend with a shoulder shrug, just as they had accepted every other unfortunate happening in their city.

If only she'd had foresight of this coming incident— she would have alighted from the bus along with the other passengers at the last scheduled bus stop. Instead, she'd chosen to stay behind because the driver had stated he would be driving farther along in her direction.

Now that she thought about it, her instincts had flared before she'd even boarded the bus in the first place, but fool that she was, she'd shrugged off the feeling upon seeing already seated passengers. How she wished she had obeyed. Right now, her instincts were blaring in alarm at the suffocating stink of danger around her, especially as the driver switched gear and drove through the busy highway as though the spirits of the undead were after him. Other buses plying their route whizzed by in a blur.

Her thoughts lay in quandary. Her salary of fifteen thousand naira as a graphics designer with a large format print company in Palmgrove proved barely enough for herself and her mother. All she had in her faded black handbag was the exact transportation fare that would ferry her home.

"Oga, please." Her voice shook, and she was pretty sure they could hear the loud staccato beats of her heart. "I don't have any money on me."

Raucous laughter followed her words, coming from the driver's direction.

"Who is interested in your change? You are the one who will bring in money for us."

A huge ball of fear unravelled in Odion's stomach, spreading its strands into every cell and tissue it could find. *Would she serve as ransom?* Another thought seized and took firm root in her mind. *Are they ritualists?*

Eyes widening, her breathing grew rapid and even more painful. Testimonies of how God had rescued people from similar situations such as this began to play in her mind, and she started to pray, hoping for that kind of miracle, too. She even recited Psalms 23.

Nothing happened. The driver's mocking chuckle drew her head back up, and as the passing light of street lamps limned his grotesque features, she shivered involuntarily.

A picture of her mother suddenly surfaced in her mind.

"Oh, Lord," she moaned. "Do not allow me to go this way. I am the present hope of my mother. How will she cope?"

The fearsome look of the conductor made her cower even more. "Shut up there. You for no kukuma enter this motor. Abi, your mind no advise you before. Nonsense!"

Odion snivelled. To think she had classified him as nice and almost handsome when he'd smiled at her earlier on. Apparently, he could switch to villain quite easily.

"That's your last warning, else I'll come and rape you over there!"

She froze at the words of the driver, and her heartbeat began to hurt, the gravity of her situation fully sinking in.

"Guy, let's enjoy her before we hand over to Baba."
His voice dripped with lust, and—

"Na fine girl sef," the bus conductor agreed, his eyes slowly raking over her form and lingering far too long on her breasts. Her hands spontaneously crossed over them, but her thick gown could not shield the rest of her from exposure. "Wait first. If she talk again, we go enjoy her for here."

She placed her palms securely over her mouth, and the only movement from her came through the uncontrollable jerking of her knees. Even her urgent need to urinate got suppressed.

As they drove farther away from the city and its bright lights into the interiors of a town ruled by rough bumpy roads and bright star light, her legs began to feel leaden, her head bigger. Catching drifts of "she dey sleep?" and "scopolamine" from the floating conversation between the driver and his conductor, she fell into a deep sleep.

***

She was wet.

The pungent smell of urine hit her nostrils as she woke to the sound of raised voices and a pounding headache. Struggling to focus her bleary eyes, she surveyed her surroundings. Trussed into a sitting position on a central pole, she could see nothing else in the small, empty woodshed except ... Was that blood? Determinedly, she turned her face away from the dark patch on the floor.

The constant trills of crickets indicated her closeness to a bush and increased her goose bumps. How could she have slept in the midst of danger? Even her tongue did not belong to her. Her lips had gone dry, swollen. *I'm sure it's not ordinary, they must have used something on me.* Something kept tugging at her memory until ... *Chai! Scopolamine.* She had heard tales of that drug used by criminals to induce deep sleep in their victims or leave them in a zombie-like state until the effects wore off. They must have sprinkled the powder on her change, she decided.

Footsteps approached, and the voices became more legible. An argument. She strained her ears to catch the words.

"Why didn't you carry your indicator? It would have saved you the stress of bringing me a wrong girl."

The voice sounded authoritative. Probably their leader.

"Baba, we forgot. What do we do? Isn't she useful in any way?"

She recognized this voice as the bus driver's.

"What! No way!" came the reply from that authoritative voice. "I don't want to carry any curse on my head."

"Make I waste am, Baba."

The deadly voice belonged to the bus conductor, and her heart lurched with fear. Were they talking about her?

"Waste who? So you can come to me for protection afterwards?" The voice supposed to be Baba's sounded pissed. "I won't help you when that time comes. If you want what's best for you, send her away. She's a twin, and we don't use them for rituals or harm them directly. It will backfire on us in so many ways."

Her brows furrowed in concentration. Were they talking about her or someone else? She had been born a twin although her twin brother had died at birth. But they couldn't have known that except ... if Baba was a juju priest.

"Bruno, go and release her," the driver said. "We'll have to scout for another girl this night."

Angry footsteps and heavy grumbling drew nearer in her direction, and her heart beats kicked up. Soon enough, the bus conductor appeared and cut the ropes around her hands and legs in so rough a manner that she was sure he'd nicked her wrists with his knife on purpose.

"Get up," he barked.

If eyes could kill, she would definitely be dead. Placing his gun on the back of her head, he instructed her to walk in front of him, and she obeyed promptly. Her jelly-like legs kept her stumbling forward 'til they approached a small opening in a dark looming forest.

The gun lifted from her head, the catch clicking. "Oya, start to dey run. If you make mistake turn back, I go shoot you."

Odion needed no further invitation before taking to her heels. She kept running without turning, afraid he was behind her. Her breaths sounded loud—could his be mixed with hers, as well—but she dared not look back. Stumbling over tree limbs, she fell many a time. Thick branches from nowhere scratched her arms, and leaves slapped her face.

Still, she kept going. She couldn't stop now, not when death loomed so close. The loud cries of the cricket and scurrying rodents in the forest darkness only served to heighten her sense of danger, and she ran without thinking of direction. Soon, her eyes caught a distant light shining from the eastern part of the forest.

"It must be a village. Dear Lord, please help me. Complete my testimony," she prayed, taking a quick look behind her. Satisfied she was alone, she lowered her pace. Giant droplets of sweat fell from her into the darkness, and her gown clung like second skin as she ran towards the light, hope beginning to bud in her breast once more.

A hand came out from nowhere and grabbed her, and the frightful scream making its way out got stuck in her throat when the cold metal of a gun barrel registered on her temple.

CHAPTER TWO

Odion Osahon

"What's your mission?" a guttural voice barked. "Who sent you? Answer me."

Fear snaked all over Odion's body, causing her to tremble like the neighbour in her compound who had palsy.

"Nobody sent me, sir," she squeaked. "Please don't kill me. I am escaping from ritualists."

"Ritualists?" The man gave a dry laugh. "Story for the birds. You must think I'm stupid, right?"

He cocked his gun to fire, and she screamed.

"Hold it," another voice commanded. A deeper one with authority. "It's possible she might just be saying the truth."

Odion's shoulders slumped with temporary relief as the gun left her head.

"Remember that hideout I told you I had discovered about eight kilometres from here," he continued. "It's possible it could be a den for ritualists, or—"

"And it's possible she could be a spy for the Black Mamba", the man still holding her fiercely.

"Be that as it may, I don't want innocent blood on our hands. She's already here. I might as well take her to the Boss. He will determine if she's a Black Mamba or not."

"Alright, then." He pushed her towards the other man, and she fell. "I'll remain here to stand guard."

The second man—her saviour—pulled her up, and she looked into his face for the first time. One word registered in her cotton-wool-filled head. *Rugged.* Her brown skinned saviour struck an imposing figure despite sharing a height of five-foot-ten with her. Well-defined muscles bulged through the shoulders of his shirt and peeped out through the open neck. She could grind pepper on that chest.

A fully shaved head and gold earring glinting from his left ear gave him a tough look, and the only hair that could be found on his face were the beginnings of a day-old beard spread across his chin. His eyes appeared deeply set and kind. Those eyes were the reason why she could breathe normally again. She suddenly became aware of her general dishabille and tugged nervously at her gown torn in four places.

He simply held her hand and said nothing, pulling her gently towards the direction she had been heading for. The light grew brighter and the path even wider as the first sightings of dawn streamed through the leaves of the forest. Her body began to ache with all the scratches and bruises she had incurred, and she struggled to walk because her legs had turned wooden. Terrifying thoughts tortured her mind. What if their boss ordered her execution? These people clearly had no trust for strangers.

Finally, they came into a cleared area where she discovered a white stone mansion bathed in light from the security bulbs surrounding it. The lights she had seen from afar, and it puzzled her to find such a beautiful building in the middle of nowhere.

Indeed, the mansion looked beautiful, fashioned after the houses of the colonial era with a staircase outside that wound to the left side of the house, and a peaked roof, slanting down at an angle that seemed to say "Welcome" to the rising sun which cast a sweet glow upon the walls.

Neatly trimmed hedges ran all around. The front porch held huge pillars with a forbidding brown mahogany door decked with bronze. Two identical clay pots of topiaries stood on both sides of the main door, but they did nothing to soften the look of the house.

The only thing marring the beauty of the environment? A dilapidated shed tucked to the right side of the building. There seemed to be no fence or gate, but rather more men armed with guns surrounding the perimeter. The ones she passed by simply gave her a blank stare and a slight nod to the man with her.

A tall, light-skinned man who seemed to be in his mid-forties emerged from the front door of the house. He bore a commanding presence enunciated by his well-trimmed goatee and serious-looking eyes. Dressed in all white, a huge gold chain dangled from his neck. It had a crucifix as pendant. Beside him stood a buxom, light-skinned lady obviously in her thirties, her boobs almost spilling from the tight brown gown on her.

"Who is she?" the man bellowed out.

The look he gave almost melted her into the ground.

"We found her on our outskirts, Boss."

"Kill her. We do not entertain strangers around here." This time, the buxom lady had spoken up.

Odion flinched. Unexpectedly, the man called 'Boss' struck the lady across her face so hard that her lips split. Odion drew back with shock. If women were handled in such manner, what would happen to her? She began to whisper what could be her last prayers as she saw his eyes literally become slits. *This man is deadly.*

Despite his obvious tremble, he deserved a medal for his ability to rein in his anger. His voice sounded calm as he waved a warning finger in the face of the buxom lady still on the floor, holding her slapped cheek.

"Do not ever speak on my behalf again. Do you understand? I am in charge here, not you." Curling his lips, he mockingly added, "Just because I give you the opportunity to grace my bed does not mean you get to speak when men are talking."

If it were another place, the feminist in her would have risen to the occasion, but at the moment, that part of her had gone into hiding.

The Boss turned his attention back to them. "What's her story, Eric?"

His name is Eric.

He thrust her forward. "She says she was escaping from ritualists. Bode seems to think she's a Black Mamba, but I figured you could tell if she actually is."

The Boss turned his full gaze on her, and she ducked her head under his observation. Long moments passed before he spoke again.

"You do realize what becomes of her now that she has seen my face, don't you?"

"I am quite aware of the consequences and would like to speak with you in confidence, if you don't mind, Boss."

"To my office, then." Turning around, he barked instructions to the buxom lady with a sneer. "Lydia, take her to the back quarters and get her cleaned up. I might as well know exactly what I'm looking at."

"Yes, Boss," Lydia coldly replied. She beckoned Odion over with a finger and simply said, "Follow me!" before moving on, not bothering to see if she had obeyed.

Odion followed her reluctantly. She knew better than to engage a spited woman.

CHAPTER THREE

Eric Francis

"No one sees me and goes scot-free. You know that very well. Why didn't you just kill her?" his boss reiterated when they were comfortably seated in his office, sharing a bottle of brandy.

Eric shrugged unaffectedly. He just had, and would never be comfortable with the shedding of innocent blood. If he said something now, it would naturally lead to their usual argument.

As if hearing his thoughts, the Boss remarked, "You and your ideals." After a pause, he added, "It's not your fault they died."

"Still, I should have called you." He pulled away from the memory constantly torturing his soul. "I may not have saved them, but I can save others."

His boss sighed. Eric thought he would pursue the conversation, but he didn't. Instead, he asked, "Has Lucy's parents been compensated?"

"Yes," came his grateful reply. "Our men took a cheque of one million naira to them yesterday."

His boss, Brian Francis, was the leader of an international drug syndicate called 'The Eye,' and the name proved fitting because they had an eye in almost every part of the world. As expected with a well-networked organization, they had enemies eager to bring them down. Putting the word out there that their headquarters sat in Togo had helped to put blood-thirsty hounds off their trail, and only friends and loyalists knew the location of this house within the forests of Badagry. Eric knew he hated losing a worker to death. For this reason, he tried to assuage his guilt by settling their families.

"You should have made it more. Lucy served us well. It's unfortunate we lost her the way we did."

He detected a sad note in the tone of his voice, but said nothing about it. The Boss obviously felt this way because

Lucy had been one of his concubines. Had he started to care for her?

"That shootout was totally unexpected. I'm still investigating it. There is more to Lydia's story than what she's telling us." He frowned, remembering Lydia's earlier display. "Speaking of her, she's becoming more possessive by the day. You need to keep an eye on that one."

"Nah", came the dismissive reply. "I can handle her."

"If you say so, Boss."

"Can you drop the 'boss' thing? It's just the two of us here."

Eric smiled while scratching the day's undergrowth on his chin.

"It's better I make it a part of me so I don't slip up in public." He really needed a shave. Downing the rest of his drink, he leaned back in the chair and crossed his feet. "I think the new girl would make a suitable replacement for Lucy. She must be brave and ingenuous to have escaped from the hands of ritualists."

"You believe the ritualist story?"

"Yes."

The Boss' eyes become clouded with thoughts as he absently drummed his fingers on the hard mahogany desk. "We'll have to train her."

"I could handle her training, if you want," he offered.

The Boss' eyebrows shot upward in surprise.

"You hardly ever train someone." He chuckled. "You can't tell me you want to bed such? She's not even much of a looker." He raised an eyebrow mockingly in question. "Has your taste changed?"

Eric grew irritated. "Who's talking about bedding her? You should know by now that I don't sleep with the ladies here."

"Yet, you slept with Maria."

He couldn't wipe the surprise off his face quickly enough, and his boss chortled with glee.

"So, you thought I wouldn't know?"

He shrugged resignedly. "It was just one time."

"True," he agreed. "But she made you break your rules. It seems you have a thing for the ladies you bring in."

"It was a stupid mistake, and we were both drunk."

"So you say, but I don't think it was a mistake on her part."

Eric stared at his boss with scepticism, but Brian gave an artless shrug.

"It's possibly the reason why she always requests jobs in far-off locations. I am only too happy to comply."

"You mean she personally requested for the mission in the Caribbean?"

The Boss nodded.

This news astounded Eric. He'd always thought he and Maria were good friends. He filed the information away, would chew over it in his quiet hour.

"Anyway," he airily said. "There's nothing attractive about this new girl. I'm sure you saw that."

"You're right, though. I wouldn't have touched her if I were in your place."

He was not comfortable with the condescending remark, but he refrained from making a statement. He couldn't change the way others think. Still, he wondered why he was so bothered about the girl. She was a stranger, after all. There was nothing to her ... except for those eyes. Doe-like and deeply pooled with innocence.

A knock sounded on the door.

"Who is it?" the Boss hollered.

"It's Lydia. I'm here with the woman."

Lydia had a soft, angelic voice which tended to have an effect on men. Sometimes, he felt she was aware and employed the information to her advantage.

"Come in."

Eric's eyes popped the moment his new girl walked in. She looked like a tantalizing vision in a long-sleeved, tight white bodycon outfit which Lydia had obviously lent her. Her old, dowdy gown had definitely been hiding a fantastic treasure. This girl had the kind of curves that appeared only in his fantasies, and those hips ...

"O Lord," escaped from his lips.

Hot blood filled his groin, and he suddenly grew hot all over. Swallowing, he tore his gaze away and fought for control. Glancing at his boss, he could clearly see he was not the only one affected, and he caught the flash of jealousy that passed through Lydia's eyes before she quickly schooled her features.

He chuckled inwardly, hardly ever missing a thing—the reason why the Boss had made him overseer. *Lydia must be cursing the fates right now for possessing only tight gowns.*

The naked lust in his boss' eyes sent a surge of protective feeling through him. *He can't have her.* He was pretty sure this lady would have been devoured right in this office if none of them had been present. It was no secret that their boss liked his sex rough, and she didn't look like his typical candidate. An aura of innocence around her screamed 'untouched.'

"You may leave us, Lydia."

Lydia obeyed with a quick nod as the Boss motioned the woman to the centre of the room. Eric could see what she saw, a tastefully furnished office with black and white linoleum floors. Walls painted white, and a huge mahogany desk placed close to the centre of the room with the Boss seated directly behind it. Her eyes lingered briefly on the bronze sculptures placed on the bookshelf, making him wonder if she loved art.

The Boss finally spoke into the loaded silence. "Tell me about yourself."

Eric noticed her hesitation for the slightest of moments before she spoke.

"My name is Odion Osahon, and I work with Premier Printing Press in Palmgrove."

Not the answer his boss needed—a familiar frown settled in the man's brow. Why did people feel their workplace provided a good description of them?

"Are your parents still alive?" the Boss asked again.

"My mother is."

"Where do you live?"

"I stay in Oshodi, sir."

The Boss nodded. "Alright, Odion. You can leave. Lydia will assign you to a room where you can rest. I'm sure you're exhausted from your adventures of the night. I'll send for you later in the evening."

Eric's eyebrows almost reached his head. The Boss was never nice nor considerate.

"Okay, sir." Odion curtsied before taking her leave.

Immediately after the door had shut after her, Eric spoke. "I know that look.

"Yeah." The Boss smiled, scratching his goatee in his familiarly contemplative way. "She definitely surprised us. I never knew a beauty would shine underneath all that dirt."

Brian sat up. "Make a research," he instructed. "Find out all you can about her. If she's a spy, I might as well enjoy her before she dies," he remarked with a grin and winked before continuing. "If she's not, then she's welcome to our world."

Suddenly, they heard a gunshot followed by an agonized scream. It sounded like the new girl.

CHAPTER FOUR

Odion Osahon

Odion lay disoriented on the ground, her left arm throbbing with hot pain. She could feel her blood seeping away and wondered if this was the way people died. Fast footsteps approached. *They're going to finish what they started.* Her fighting spirit was well depleted. She simply closed her eyes to await her fate.

Rough arms pulled her up, forcing her to open her eyes. One of the guards loomed over her.

"There's no need for all this drama. It's just a flesh wound," he said. "If Madam Lydia wanted to kill you, she would have. It's plain and simple."

He then dragged her back to the mansion.

She no longer cared. What more could they do?

Earlier on, she had tried escaping when Lydia had been distracted. Remaining here among these criminals would be dangerous for her. She had not missed the looks from this organization's leader, and for a minute, she had thought he would jump on her. Even the Eric guy had not been left out. No one here could or would save her. No one.

The Boss and Eric were waiting at the entrance of the house, along with Lydia, as she approached. Eric's face looked solemn while Lydia bounced on her feet with a wide smile on her face.

A faint feeling stole over her, and she realised her left arm was bloody and soaked. She fully leaned on the guard now.

Closing her eyes, she heard the leader's cold voice.

"How bad is she, Lydia?"

"It's just a flesh wound, Boss. I had to stop her."

"A wound that obviously has to be taken care of."

Inwardly, she relaxed. *Thank God for this man. He's nice.*

"I can see she has gotten her punishment already, but still, she needs to get a taste of what happens around here when one tries to escape. Get the whip."

Whip? Had she heard right?

The guard holding her impatiently carried her back to the edge of the forest. Another guard came with a rope which he used to tie her securely to a tree trunk. The rope was the only thing stopping her from sinking to her knees.

She heard a singing sound and then, "Aaaaaiiiii! Mummy!"

Her agonized scream vibrated through the forest

Her back was on fire. She had never felt anything like this before, not even when she'd been flogged by Mr. Okafor, the strictest teacher in her secondary school. It felt like an open wound mixed with ground *atarado* pepper.

Another lash fell on her, fierier than the first. It wound around her waist and pulled off flesh.

"Jesus!"

The third landed almost immediately, and she could almost swear her bone had cracked. This was no whipping but an assault on her flesh and bones. She lost count after the fifth. This must obviously be the fire and brimstone preached about by her pastor.

When she finally thought death had come knocking, the ropes were loosened from her, and she dropped to the floor. The rays of the morning sun tortured her back even more. On the edge of blackness, she smelt the familiar perfume of the leader.

He pulled her head back and spoke into her ear. "The next time you try to escape, my men will take their turns with you. So, you had better watch it, little girl."

As he dropped her head roughly, she heard him say, "Get the doctor to administer to her wounds, Lydia. I have to go for a meeting. You're in charge until I return."

"Yes, Boss."

She felt herself being carried away, and the cool draft of an air conditioner meant she had entered a room. Voices filtered in and out of her consciousness, and one of them sounded angry. Gentle fingers prodded her wounds, making her whimper. He smelt like a doctor.

In-house doctor?

She was too weak to think, and as the prodding continued, she succumbed into the cordial darkness.

CHAPTER FIVE

Eric Francis

Five a.m. was his best hour of the day. The house remained usually quiet except for the patrolling guards on duty. Sounds of machinery would not come on until seven a.m., and only his footsteps could be heard now. He headed for the forest, far from the sightings of the house, but not in too deeply. He climbed his favourite tree and sat on his favourite bough, just like he always did since the time he'd discovered this spot at the age of ten.

This was the only time he could indulge himself with the music of the birds singing sweet soulful tunes that sounded like calls and responses. When he was younger, he would fake interpretations of the birds' songs with words like, "It's going to be a fine day," or "A good morning, beautiful sun."

Resting his back against the trunk, he closed his eyes and welcomed the morning dew as it clung to his skin and fell on his head. His mother used to call them the blessings of Heaven.

Despite the serenity of the morning, his mind was far from peaceful. Thoughts of Odion would not leave him and had tormented him through the night. The Boss had made him break one of his principles. Until yesterday, he had never hit a woman.

In Odion's case, it had been worse. He had whipped her. Remembering the mangled mess he had left as her back caused him to squirm. The whip used? Not the usual type in the market. It was very long and specially designed with sharp stones tied to the edges of each thong, meant to sting and split skin. Not a woman's, though. From the time he had joined the organization, a woman had never been whipped, only rebellious male workers, and the last time it happened had been five years ago.

Why would he have her whipped?

He sighed and dropped down, his feet guiding him where they wanted. He found her door ajar and entered. Dr. Seyi had fallen sound asleep in the plush armchair by her bedside. As for her, she came awake at the moment he stepped into her room. Probably a light sleeper. As the fog of sleep cleared from her eyes, fear entered in its place. This made him pause in his movement.

"Why did you leave the door open?" he softly asked so as not to wake the good doctor. "Mosquitoes can come in."

Mosquitoes? Really? Was that why he was here?

The good doctor stirred. So much for not wanting to disturb his sleep.

"Eric." A warm, welcoming smile spread from Dr. Seyi's lips to his eyes, seemingly seeking a response.

Eric couldn't help but return it. The good doctor always had that effect, not just on him but on other members of The Eye, including their boss. You couldn't be sad or grumpy for long around him, with him being such a happy soul. He had always been here from the time Eric had joined the organization and had always looked like this—slightly chubby, with plenty of white hair. The only difference were the lines on his angular face which had deepened as the years passed.

Doctor Seyi had helped him through his nightmares when he'd first come to live here and had tended to his injuries during training as a teenager. He felt like their father figure, and yet, no one knew anything about his past or where he came from. The Boss never spoke about it, either. Doctor Seyi was simply there.

"Good morning, sir. I came to see how she is faring."

"Why didn't you stop them from whipping me?" Her voice rang very low but clear in the quiet of the room.

Her question tore at his insides, making his guilt drive up to his throat.

The doctor sat beside her and patted her hand. "Let's not talk about that now, my child. Your focus should be on getting better."

But she shook her head, clearly not dissuaded.

"I almost died, and he just stood there." Tears glistened from her eyes. "I thought you were different."

He could lie now and nobody would tell her otherwise, but did he want to? He raised his head up. "I did the whipping, Odion."

For a minute, no sound could be heard in the room except the loud ticking of a clock.

Then, she turned to the doctor. "Please, ask him to leave."

He left before the doctor had even asked. No point in hanging around. He would never beg for a woman's company, and besides, he had a lot of work cut out for the day.

Still, he had someone deliver some chocolates and ice cream to her room by midday.

CHAPTER SIX

Odion Osahon

Shadows of the night had begun approaching her window when she finally awoke. The drug administered by the doctor had made her sleep through the day, and now, she felt well-rested and … hungry.

Doctor Seyi seemed to have anticipated her hunger because a tray with a covered bowl of food sat on the table close to her bed. It seemed he never left her bedside. He was always there when she fell asleep or woke, his smile a constant she could count on in this horrible place. Most importantly, he reminded her of home.

Her nose wrinkled with distaste. "What's that foul smell?"

"It's the salve I rubbed on your back."

"Why does it smell like shit?"

"The shitty smelling salve is the reason why you can sit up now. Besides, the Boss needs you to recover quickly."

"I am not recovering for that animal," she spat out.

Doctor Seyi simply smiled. "Destiny placed you here for a reason, and right now, you are at the mercy of that animal whether you like it or not."

"It is not my destiny to be here. The God I serve will surely deliver me."

As the words left her mouth, her thoughts assailed her. *Why didn't God help you escape yesterday? Why did he transfer you from frying pan to fire?*

"May it happen according to your faith, but while you're here, you can choose to swim with the tide or decidedly sink. It's all up to you." Placing the tray on her lap, he instructed firmly, "Now, eat."

She didn't even need to be told. As the sweet aroma of the goat meat pepper soup assailed her nostrils, her stomach rumbled.

"By the way, Eric sent down some chocolate and ice cream earlier in the day. Try to appreciate it when next you see him."

"I don't want anything from him."

"I was hoping you would say that." Chuckling, he pulled out a packet of Cadbury chocolate and a medium-sized bowl of ice cream. Her favourite brand and flavour: Fan Ice Vanilla.

"There shall be no loss," he said with such obvious glee as he dug into the ice cream while she watched with suppressed envy. "By the time you spend some time here, you'll learn to appreciate chocolate and ice cream. They are very scarce."

Scarce? "Why? They're not expensive."

He popped a square of chocolate into his mouth and then closed his eyes in obvious delight before answering. "You can only get them in town, but most of the men hardly have ice cream on their minds when returning from missions."

She focused on her food and tried to ignore his gluttonous display.

Halfway through her meal, the doctor spoke up again. "I'm going to give you some advice, you can take it or leave it. While you're here, try to make friends. It's best if you get decent ones like Eric on your side."

She rolled her eyes. "How do you know he's decent?"

His brows knitted into a tight frown. "Are you questioning my judgement of character?"

"I'm sorry, sir. Didn't mean it that way."

"If another person had done the whipping in his place, you would not be alive. If anything, be grateful to him even if it doesn't look like you should. The whip used on you was designed for the brawny back of a man and not the soft flesh of a woman." His face reddened as his tone picked up. "I don't know what Brian was thinking when he made that order. I thought we had put a stop to that barbaric act."

"Is Brian the name of the leader?"

The doctor nodded.

Odion suddenly felt tired and full. She had drunk her pepper soup to the last spoon. The cook who'd prepared it had done a good job. All the spices had blended well, and the meat had been tender.

"I really enjoyed my meal, sir. Thank you so much." She rested against her pillows, struggling to keep her eyes open.

"It's time for bed, my daughter." He tucked her in gently.

Tears sprang to her eyes at his gesture, and she wondered if he had children of his own. *I'll ask him tomorrow.*

She yawned. "Goodnight, sir."

* * *

Three days later, Eric came visiting again.

"Doctor Seyi insisted that I look in on you. He had to go on an urgent business with the Boss."

"Well, as you can see, I am fine."

Nodding, he turned to leave. "Do you need anything?"

Her spontaneous reply was 'No!' but her insides warred with 'Ice cream.' The memory of Doctor Seyi consuming her ice cream had still not left her.

He seemed to notice her hesitation because the look of kind concern he bestowed on her almost made her weep. "Are you sure?"

She ducked her head, suddenly unable to meet his eyes. "Well, if there's some ice cream, I don't mind having some."

She could hear the smile in his voice when he said, "I'll send someone down."

The doctor's words rang in her head. *It's best if you get decent ones like Eric on your side.*

Her palms tightened under the duvet. "You could come instead, if you want. It would be nice to know you more."

He said nothing and left but did come back and every day after that. Sometimes, he spent thirty minutes with her, and other days, he would stay up to two hours. She began to look forward to their conversations. They talked about politics, fame, women's rights, and even her love for art. She told him about her job as a graphics designer and her dreams of owning her own printing company where her designs would no longer be stifled.

Her tone turned wistful. "Will I ever be allowed to go home again?"

He didn't have the right answer for her and simply said, "You're alive right now. Let that count."

CHAPTER SEVEN

Odion Osahon

"Get ready. You'll be taking some of our products across the border. Try not to get caught."

Lydia had delivered the cold message in the early hours of the morning, causing her thoughts to spiral in various confused directions. She wasn't a baby and had discovered through her conversations with the doctor that this place was a drug syndicate.

If she carried their product, it would make her a drug courier, and if she didn't, she would be in danger of being killed. The warnings of this organization's leader penetrated her dreams. She shivered. Yes, she would do anything to protect her own virtue, but would it be at the detriment of her values and all that she stood for? She was torn with her mind going round and round in circles until the effects of the drugs she had been given earlier took over and drifted her off into sleep.

By nine a.m., she had been given a heavy satchel bag which she didn't bother to open. She had dressed in a bright green T-shirt and tight black jeans that melded with her skin. They had also come from Lydia with her unsurprising complaints: "We'll need to do some shopping for you. You can't keep wearing my clothes. You'll only end up ruining them."

Odion had rolled her eyes and stuck a tongue out at her when she wasn't looking.

She was directed to a blue Peugeot 406—the 2004 model—she would travel in along with another member of the organization. But before she got into the car, Lydia gave her final instructions.

"The driver has all the details. All you have to do is smile and look pretty when you are handing the products over to our partners."

She nodded in acquiescence, got in, and the driver took off. They travelled in silence for an hour before they approached the border, and she was surprised to discover she had been in Badagry all of this time.

On getting close to the first checkpoint at Badagry, the police flagged their vehicle down and asked for their papers. Hope suddenly stared at her in the face, and a light began to fill her heart. Quickly, she alighted and addressed one of the police officers there.

"Please, I need to speak with your Oga."

"Anything?"

"It's urgent I speak with him."

He bellowed out to another officer seated in a patrol car. "Oga, this lady here wan discuss with you ooo."

"Bring her here."

The policeman led her to the patrol car parked to one side of the road. An elderly and tall, dark-skinned and well-built policeman sat in it. From the insignia on his uniform, he was an Inspector, and his name tag read Shola Waheed. Closer to him, she found his deep voice soothing and fatherly. *His voice must be the reason he was accepted into the police force.* Obviously, he had experienced a lot in life.

"How can I help you, young lady?" he asked.

Gazing at the white hairs dotting his temple, she felt safe and secure. *This is someone I can trust.*

"Sir, I need to report a crime. I am being forced by a drug syndicate to carry hard drugs over the border. I felt I should report this as a law-abiding citizen of this country."

"Do you have evidence?"

"Yes, sir. One of them is in that car waiting for me. You can also find the drugs, too. They're in a bag."

He looked at the car and studied the driver very well.

"You have done the right thing. What's your name?"

"I'm Odion Osahon."

"Alright. Let me make a quick call, and then, we can head to the station."

"Alright, sir. Thank you so much."

When he'd finished, he motioned her into the Peugeot. "Let's head to the station so you can make your statement."

Odion smiled as relief flooded through her heart. He believed her. At a point when he had been on the phone, she had begun to regret her decision because the drugs in her possession could be termed as hers, and that would only sink her into deeper trouble.

She was finally safe. "Okay, sir. Thank you so much. God bless you for this."

"It's no problem, Madam. I'm only fulfilling my duty," he replied.

Inspector Waheed got into the car and ordered the driver into the back seat. The man complied without any resistance. After shouting out instructions to the other policemen, he drove off.

***

Odion was surprised to see the inspector drive towards the big house in the forest without anyone giving him a description or even having backup. How could he just go straight into the lion's den alone? Something about this was not right. Even Ike, The Eye's driver, looked unconcerned for someone supposedly going to jail. Was this a setup? She suddenly felt uneasy.

"Excuse me, sir. Won't you call for backup?"

"My men are already waiting there. I called them before we left."

"Oh!" *That's what that call had been all about.*

"Have you been there before? You seem to know your way."

"I know the house quite well. I just have not had enough evidence with which to nail their leader. Thanks to you, all that has changed."

She smiled and relaxed in her seat, feeling proud of herself. Something made her turn back, and she caught Ike grinning. This confused her. Something was definitely up. She remembered Lydia boasting that the eye of the organization was everywhere, hence the reason for their name.

Could Lydia have been saying the truth? Was the inspector under the pay of The Eye? She shook her head. It couldn't be. The inspector looked like an upstanding fellow. She considered herself a fair judge of character and concluded he was definitely not a crook. End of story. Besides, criminals in the movies usually smiled when being arrested, and this guy was not different. She leaned back in her seat and closed her eyes in anticipation of freedom.

They got to the house soon enough, but strangely, she could find no police cars around. *They are probably hiding undercover.*

Inspector Waheed steered her and Ike towards the main house. He definitely knew his way around. The guards stared at them but couldn't do anything as they walked past, and a feeling of exhilaration rushed through her. She felt powerful walking side by side with the inspector and would always relish this feeling.

The police inspector ushered her and the driver into the leader's office, and they came face to face with him. He had a huge smile plastered on his face. Eric was there, too.

"Welcome! Welcome, Inspector Waheed! You have done well today."

"Thank you, Boss," the inspector replied.

CHAPTER EIGHT

Eric Francis

Eric stared balefully at the retreating back of the policeman, even though he could not really blame him. If he had not turned Odion in, he would have died in her place. It was just the way things worked, especially with a witness like Ike involved. The man's wife had just given birth, and the safety of his family would be more important than that of a stranger.

The penalty for informants meant death, and he knew this more than anyone because he had taken out a few guys for this transgression.

Stubborn woman. She had fooled him into thinking she wanted to blend in. He had even begun to think that she cared for him and they could maybe have a future together. But her actions today had bathed him with reality. She wanted nothing to do with this place, including him.

Still, he wouldn't stand around to watch her die. He still felt sick to the stomach at the pain he had caused her with his hands, and though Doctor Seyi had assured him the scars would fade off with time, the assurance hadn't wiped the memory of her bloodied back on that fateful morning.

He could not really state exactly what he found special about Odion. Yes, she was beautiful, but not the first he had seen or dated. It was something else. Something that made him feel a sense of peace whenever he was with her, like there still existed some hope for his very dark soul.

He hurried back to his uncle's office while preparing himself mentally for the altercation they would have. He would save her come hell or high water.

***

He could hear her muted screams through the brown ebony door of his uncle's office. Without knocking, he barged in, taking in the scene. Odion knelt on her knees crying copiously while the Boss advanced towards her with a murderous look in his eyes.

Odion ran to him, holding on to his knees and begging.

"Please, help me beg him. I made a vow to God that I would remain a virgin until marriage." She started hiccupping, "I don't want to take off my clothes."

"Get out." The Boss spoke in that tone he hated, as though he were a pesky house fly.

Hardening his resolve, he stood his ground. "No."

Shock registered on the Boss' face, so much so that the redness in his eyes immediately lessened as they stared at each other across the space of the office. All through childhood and even 'til now, he had never disobeyed him, not even once.

The puzzled look in his eyes disappeared, and the light of knowledge replaced it. "You dare to disobey me because of her?"

His voice was calm, but Eric understood the coming storm they belied. Respectfully, he bowed his head to reply in a low tone, "I do not want you to kill her."

The Boss waved him into a seat, taking his place behind his desk.

"She said she's a virgin."

Eric drew back in consternation and looked at Odion again. Who would have thought she was one? She never even acted like one. *How do virgins behave?* He shook his head. She made quite a sorry sight on her knees. Was that mucus running freely from her nose?

"What do you think?"

He knew the answer the Boss expected, but ... "She might be saying the truth. Let's get the doctor to check her."

The Boss nodded, his brows drawn, biting the side of his right cheek like he always did when mulling over a matter. Finally, he leaned back in his chair and summoned Odion to the table by crooking his right forefinger. He gave her a hard stare. "Do you understand the consequences of lying to me?"

"I'm not lying, sir," she sobbed.

"So you're a virgin, right?"

"Yes, sir." She nodded.

"It's 'Boss' to you."

"Yes, Boss."

He then turned to Eric. "Take her to the doctor. I need the results in an hour."

***

An hour later, Odion's report lay on the table. She had spoken the truth.

He had been so worried for her. However, he couldn't relax yet. The smile on the Boss' face meant he was up to something. He just knew it.

The man brought out a folder from his drawer, and he recognized it instantly—the same folder containing information he had gathered about her. The Boss smiled at Odion in the exact same way Tom did when he had Jerry confused in his favourite cartoon series. Suddenly, he feared for her.

His boss picked up his phone and dialled a number, and a voice came through the speaker after the third ring. "Hello?"

The shock on Odion's face could not be described. He knew who was at the other end of the line—her mother.

After several "Hellos?", the Boss ended the call. His smile grew even wider.

"You are surprised, right? It's obvious you have no value for your life, but I'm sure you'll be concerned enough for your mother. Presently, I have her watched. I believe Number 8, Afariogun Street in Oshodi is familiar?"

His insides turned, bringing his old fears back to surface. Having a family was dangerous. Memories of his parents assaulted him with force now. It had been nineteen years since that fateful incident, but the smell of their blood had still not departed from underneath his nostrils.

"Please, sir ... Boss," she stuttered. "I'll do anything you want. Do not harm my mother, I beg of you."

She didn't have a choice. The Boss had her where he wanted. She would be a puppet like the others now.

His eyes jumped open when the Boss banged on the desk with excitement.

"Music to my ears. That's what I like to hear. I knew you would come around eventually." He turned to Eric, exuberance lighting up his face. "Give her a crash course on how to shoot this week. You are the only one I can trust to handle this. She'll deliver a message to Kolawole Amoo at Eko Hotel next week. That will be all."

He sputtered, "Kolawole Amoo? She lacks the experience for that."

"She's the only virgin who has come our way, and we are not missing out on this opportunity," the Boss returned, his eyes flaming.

Lydia had once been sent to kill Kolawole Amoo, the leader of a rival organization called Black Mamba. She had not succeeded, the only mission she had ever failed. Her bullets had not been able to penetrate the man due to a strong impenetrable charm he used as a shield against bullets. She had been lucky to escape alive. Her investigations had revealed the man could only be killed by a virgin. Since the past year, they had been stuck. Virgins hardly joined the mafia.

"Even if she's the one to do the job, how do you expect her to learn how to shoot in one week?" Eric was confounded. "Are you trying to get her killed?"

"She does not have to be an expert shot," the Boss quipped back. "If all falls according to plan, she'll be shooting at close range."

Eric kept quiet.

Brian stood up, a way of dismissing them.

"Send Lydia to me. She'll serve as a substitute since this madam here has dedicated her virginity to God," he added with a mocking tone.

Eric turned to Odion. "We might as well get started. There's a lot of catching up to do."

CHAPTER NINE

Odion Osahon
"Focus on your sight alignment."

Eric guided her gun hand in the direction of the large dummy used as target, but she couldn't focus. How could she when his warm breath tickled her ear and her body fit snugly into his, arm to arm, bum to groin, soft thigh to tough one? She felt a sense of completeness with him around her and closed her eyes to savour the delicious sensations bombarding her being.

"Place your legs astride," he continued, touching her thighs in the process. "And lean into it."

"Now, shoot."

He pulled back from her, crashing her back to reality. Her body protested against the disconnection, but her arms obeyed his instructions.

He had spent the last three hours instructing her on gun safety, its handling, and how to disassemble and reassemble the pieces. They were practising in the basement of the house which she never even knew existed. The house was definitely full of surprises.

The basement held a shooting range bathed in light from numerous white fluorescent bulbs inserted in the ceiling. It had six pistol lanes with shooting targets placed twenty-five yards away from the shooting point outlined by a thick yellow line drawn across the floor and which she was not supposed to cross. In each lane, a large placard shaped into human form had been painted and placed on an iron stand which served as the shooting targets.

She squeezed the trigger, and the recoil from the gun pushed her back. The bullet went two feet off the dummy.

"Not bad for a first timer," he remarked, sounding impressed.

The shadow of a smile dotted his lips before disappearing into his previously cold, drawn countenance. *What was he angry with her for?* Apart from drumming out instructions, he had refused to engage her in any form of conversation, and she was fed up with his attitude.

"Look, I couldn't just sit around and do nothing."

"And I thought you had some sense," he drawled out in an insulting tone.

This got her riled up. "I have plenty of sense, and that is the reason why I will not give up on getting out of this hellhole."

"At the risk of your mum?"

She had no answer for him.

"Like I said, I thought you had some sense."

Her insides roiled, but she chose to stay quiet.

He strode to the end of the hall and spoke loudly from there. "I think it's time you select your gun. Come and find the one that works best for you."

She frowned, puzzled, and held up the revolver in her hand. "What's wrong with this one?"

"Nothing's wrong, but you might find another you prefer more."

Getting to where he stood, she discovered an assortment of guns displayed on the wall right behind the wide entrance doors of the basement. The guns here looked sophisticated and completely different from the ones she used to see on TV. These mafia people were really equipped.

She pointed at a rifle that looked like the ones she had seen in movies. "That one."

Eric burst out laughing. "Are you for real? You don't even have the muscles for it. Pick something small."

"Why must I pick a small gun? Are you looking down on me?"

"Me?" His brows drew upwards incredulously, and his eyes took on a twinkle. "Look down on you? Who am I to look down on our escaper of the year?"

"Sha, bring the gun for me."

"No. You can't handle it yet. You're still new to shooting. Besides, you've got small hands."

She snorted. He was just giving excuses.

"You don't believe me, right? Okay." He placed his handgun in her hands. "That's a Magnum .35. If you can shoot five rounds successfully with it, then you can choose the rifle and any other gun you want."

She smiled. "Fair deal."

His gun felt heavy, but she didn't complain as she raised it up with both of her hands. There was nothing to it. All she had to do was pull the trigger.

"Make sure your fingers are off the trigger until you're pointing at the target," Eric warned.

She stood astride, planted the balls of her feet firmly into the ground, her knees slightly bent, and fired.

"Aaaii!" she hollered and jumped, waving her ringing palms in the air one after the other. The recoil from her revolver had been nowhere close to this one.

Angrily, she faced Eric. "Why didn't you tell me it hurts like this?"

He shrugged carelessly. "I tried, but you were not listening. I figured you would understand better through experience."

She rolled her eyes. "Yes, yes, you are right and I am wrong. Now, can we look through the small guns you were talking about?"

He smiled and shook his head. "Are we going to argue like this all the time?"

She took up a mock-serious look. "Where's the fun without our arguments?"

They both laughed.

Wagging his fingers in her direction, all he said was, "You."

It seemed the ice between them had thawed.

He showed her an array of guns with unfamiliar names like Glock 43 9mm or, according to him, a .38 Smith and Wesson Special. None of them mattered to her until she gripped the one called Sig Sauer P238. The moment she held it, she felt a kinship with it.

Smiling, she looked at Eric. His eyes were twinkling, too. He understood.

"She is mine."

***

"Alright! Let's wrap it up for today."

She was glad to hear that. Her arms protested heavily, especially the left, each time she lifted a dumbbell, and she seriously doubted if she could lift her arms anymore. She couldn't even feel them. So much for building her upper body strength.

Despite the coolness of the basement, she was sweating profusely, and as she put away the dumbbells, she became aware of her itching back. The bandaged part of her arm had not been left out.

Eric seemed to notice her discomfort because he asked, "Are you alright?"

She nodded, but it didn't convince him. His eyes turned hooded as they ran over her.

"I'll take you to your room. You need to rest."

"Why are you so nice to me?" she blurted out, and then cringed inwardly as her mother's warnings played in her ear. She always expressed half-formed thoughts without thinking them through, and her mum had often warned that the trait would get her into a lot of trouble.

"Honestly, I don't know." He didn't seem put off by her question. In fact, he was looking up to the sky as if in search of an answer there. "Is it a crime to be nice to you?" he teased.

She grinned.

They had gone halfway to her room when the sound of running footsteps made them turn around. She recognized the fellow coming—the barrel-chested guy who had picked her up from the ground after she had been shot by Lydia.

Eric immediately became alert and business-like. "Martins, what is the problem?"

"It's Bode." Martins panted unevenly. "He and Paul are threatening to blow each other's head off."

"Paul?" His eyes almost popped. "Let's go."

"What about her?"

"She's coming, too," he threw off-handedly as he hurried back.

Martins' big eyeballs widened, and Odion thought the pupils would pop.

"But ..."

Eric stopped and faced Martins square in the face.

"She's one of us now," he replied in a tone that brooked no further argument, and Martins wisely clamped his lips shut.

One would think a man of Martin's size would not be so intimidated by a spare-looking fellow like Eric. Obviously, he had more going on for him than his looks.

They walked in companionable silence towards an abandoned-looking shed in front of a derelict bungalow totally removed from the house and at the edge of the forest. She was surprised to discover she had not taken note of the structure in all of her time here.

The roof of the shed hung so low, they had to duck before entering. On getting to the door of the bungalow, Martins pulled the panel, and it opened smoothly without a squeak. As they ran down the steps, Odion was surprised to find a well-lit, wide and spacious room. It led into a very long corridor with steel doors on opposite sides that ran the length of it.

To think that something like this existed underground proved baffling to her senses. How did they construct an edifice such as this? *The architect sabi work.* Even the ceiling had been plastered white and tight and had A/C vent holes in them set one metre square from each other.

The effect was very cooling and a bit too much for her. Unfortunately, she didn't have any control over it like the one in her room. It seemed the organization had a penchant for the colour white because all of the interior here also seemed bathed in white.

Loud, threatening sounds came from the fifth door on the right which lay open, and when they approached, she took in the scene. Two tall and beefy-looking men had their guns pointed at each other and were equally matched physically.

She knew the voice of the older one, though. In fact, the memory of his voice could never be wiped out of her head. She simply had a face to match it now: the one who had almost killed her when she had been running from those ritualists.

All over the room sat various stacks of yam with some even taller than her five-foot-ten frame. Quite a number of men occupied the space, too, about fifteen or more, and it seemed they had all been in the middle of stacking yams before the confrontation because some held yams in their hands. They all stood in a wide circle around the disputing men.

"Drop your guns!"

This came from Eric who had walked into the centre of the circle while she stayed on the periphery. The older man obeyed, but as the younger one turned his head to explain, Eric shot him in his left arm.

Odion jumped with fear. It had happened so fast, she had not even seen him pull out his gun now in his hands.

"Whenever I give an order, obey before explanations," he simply stated as the other man grabbed his arm and groaned in pain, his gun forgotten on the floor.

She understood his pain as her left arm throbbed lightly in reminder. Every other person in the room, about fifteen men or more, remained immobile.

Eric then faced one of them. "What happened?

Pointing to the older guy and gesticulating, he explained, "Bode caught him trying to make a phone call, and when he tried to stop him, Paul pulled out his gun."

"I see," came Eric's cold remark. "With which phone?"

"His phone," the one called Bode answered.

"My mother is seriously sick," Paul bellowed with pain

"Still, you know the rules," Eric roared back, eyes blazing. "You can only call with your phone when you're not within Badagry. Otherwise, there are safe phones you can use. You know this, yet you choose to be stubborn. Are you trying to sabotage our security?"

Without warning, he shot Paul in the right thigh. "And that's for disrespecting Bode. He has spent longer years in this organization, and that makes him your superior."

Turning to the rest in the room, he warned, "And the same applies to the rest of you. The older ones are never to be disrespected. They have earned every inch of their survival here."

He strode to the groaning Paul who sat on the floor all bloodied, stood over him threateningly, and spoke in a low voice.

"You're still useful, else I would have shot your gun arm." Beckoning on Martins, he ordered, "Take him to the doctor."

Nodding in Bode's direction, Eric walked out without sparing anyone a glance, and Odion did not wait for further instructions before following. He led her farther down the corridor, and as their footsteps echoed along, she studied him from behind.

He was a dark-skinned specimen with a lean, wiry frame that belied strength. You could pick these hints from the bunched-up muscles on his broad shoulders and his strides, quick and purposeful. Why, even his tight butt testified to the obvious fact that he worked out regularly, and though they shared the same height, he still seemed bigger than her.

Finally, they came to the last room on the left of the corridor, and she walked into it after he opened and held the door for her.

Eric seemed to relax visibly when he had shut the door behind them and even became human again by trying to give her a watery smile.

"I'm sorry you had to witness that."

She simply shrugged. With the kind of things she had seen and heard in this past week, she doubted if anything could shock her anymore. Still, it was nice to know there still existed a gentleman in him.

The room was clean and utilitarian, consisting of a bed, chair, table, and a wardrobe. A three-tiered plastic basket sat beside his bed, where he dropped in sparse personal effects. Aside from these items, the room boasted of nothing else, and its strict cleanliness unnerved her.

The picture of a laughing couple carrying a smiling child adorned the top layer of the basket, and she walked over to pick it up. The warm happiness radiating from the picture made her wonder if she would ever be happy again. Saddened, she turned back to Eric.

"Who are they?"

"My parents," came the clipped answer.

She grew curious, but the look on his face brooked no further questions.

"Have some pain relief drugs."

He was obviously trying to change the subject.

She gladly received them. "Thank you."

The itching on her back seemed to have skyrocketed in the coolness of his room.

After taking them, he opened his wardrobe and brought out a container. "Here, rub this shea butter over your back. It will help your back heal faster."

Sudden tears sprouted from her eyes. Memories spilled from the container in his hands. Shea butter was her mother's solution to any injury or cold. She missed her so much.

And now, she had grown tired of processing thoughts or events, or her attraction to this kind man. She had grown tired of doing the right thing. She *was* tired.

Not wanting to think, she lay on his bed, raised up her shirt, and unclipped her bra. "Please help me apply it."

Yes, she was not thinking at all.

CHAPTER TEN

Eric Francis

Eric lost mobility and speech as he gazed at the back offered to him. *Was she trying to seduce him?* Then, he remembered her virginity report and shook his head.

Large welts ran across her back in mismatched patterns, and it sickened him. They had starting to fade, but still looked prominent. Finally, he moved to the bed when he realised she'd meant her statement.

As he gently smeared the cream over her scars, she shivered slightly but said nothing. The softness of her skin sent heat to his head, and he paused to take a cupful of deep breath. She was not the first woman he had touched, and he didn't understand why he would be affected by a mere back as if he were a randy school boy.

Scooping out more butter, he smeared another untouched area of her back. This time, his hands sank along with the cream into the softness of her skin. They glided over her back now, worshiping every crevice and scar. He had no control over them and could only watch as though from afar while they slowly snaked their way upward and around to her breasts.

He almost lost his senses when she said, "I'm guessing my breasts are an extension of my back?" in a voice that belied the effect his ministrations were having on her before she adjusted for him to continue.

Her breasts were as soft as raw cotton, succulent and full, and as he stroked her perky nipples deftly, her breathing deepened. This further heated his head and fuelled his loins. He didn't want to think about it. He couldn't even if he wanted to. The fog of desire cloaking him tightly proved much too strong.

To think that he would be the first man with her almost maddened him. Joining her on the bed, his eyes fell on his gun staring mockingly from the table, and his fevered hands stilled.

What had he almost done? How could he have forgotten about her mission?

Cursing under his breath, he regretfully extricated himself and picked his gun from the table. Not trusting himself to look at her, he threw the words, "Try to catch some sleep," before stepping out and locking the door behind him.

CHAPTER ELEVEN

Odion Osahon

Hot shame flooded the length of Odion's body, and for a minute, she didn't move.

He had obviously found her breasts to be too flabby for his taste. Everything had come to a halt after he'd held them. All at once, she hated her breasts, her body, and her skin. Tears trickled out of her eyes, and before long, they graduated into a storm of heavy sobs.

What was she thinking? Who cared about how a man saw her? She had almost broken her vow with God. All because of a handsome face with ebony skin, the embodiment of her dream man. Was it because he had been nice to her? How could she allow a criminal like him to touch her and have encouraged him, at that? She didn't know who she was anymore.

"Help me, Lord," she cried. "I'm confused and don't even know where my head is anymore. Right every wrong in my life, and save me from this hellhole. You are the only one I have, and I remain your daughter. Protect me and my mum. I humbly ask in the name of Jesus Christ."

She couldn't exactly say when, but a certain peace slowly stole over her being before she succumbed into a deep sleep. She didn't even stir when Eric came to collect her two hours later. He decided to let her be.

Even the bravest warriors needed their rest.

CHAPTER TWELVE

Odion Osahon
"I hope we are not keeping others from sleeping."
"Not at all. This place is sound proof."
Eric had been teaching her for two hours now, and they had only just taken a break.

She was grateful for the ear plugs he had given her because her ears were still ringing from the shots even with the plugs in them. He had really been good and patient with her, and she felt comfortable and at ease around him like she had known him for a long time.

"How long have you been with The Eye?"
"Since my childhood days."
She raised her head in surprise at his relaxed form on the floor. "Childhood? You mean The Eye recruits children, too?"

"Oh, no. Don't get me wrong. We don't. I was the exception, but I'm not willing to go into that story," he replied and removed the smoking gun from her right palm. Tingling relief spread deliciously through as he sat up to massage it before continuing. "Let's talk about you. It's only a few, select ladies in our organization who go on missions like this. We call them our Messengers."

"What a corny name."
"Not when you have to deliver The Boss' message to his enemies before they die."
"What kind of message?"
He looked at her as if the answer was too obvious. "The message of death, of course."

Her turn to look shocked. "So, I am a hired assassin."

"You're not exactly hired, you know." He chuckled with a twinkle in his eyes, and she couldn't help but join in despite the absurdity of the whole situation.

"How many messengers operate here?"

"One of them is in the Caribbean right now, and the other in South Africa. Another is in Calabar. Then, we have you and Lydia here."

"Lydia?"

"Of course, Lydia, and she has never missed a shot or failed in an assignment. She was trained by The Boss himself." He paused for a brief moment. "Honestly, I feel it's too soon for you to take up a job like this, but the Boss knows best."

She curled her lips at the mention of that disgusting man. "He's such an evil man."

"Hush! Don't ever say that again."

"Well, he is. Look at all he has put me through."

The enormity of her circumstances rested heavily on her shoulders more than ever, and she began to cry.

Eric wrapped her in a soft embrace, and she felt comfort in those tough arms. Revelling in his strength and scent, she could not explain how their lips found each other. It looked as though her lips had found their missing half; they locked on to his and refused to leave.

Intense heat began to build up and spread to different parts of her body, especially heavier at her core and familiar.

He will jump off just like he did earlier.

Odion broke off the kiss and glared. "I can't believe I did that with you, not after what happened in your room and the way you jumped off."

Oops. She wished she could cut her tongue off right now—always saying stuff she was not supposed to say. She bent her head away shyly.

Eric lifted her chin until she looked straight into his brown eyes. She could see warmth and something undefinable swimming in their depths.

"I'm deeply attracted to you, Odion, and if I had not jumped off when I did, you would be pregnant by now."

Her eyes widened. She had clearly not thought of that. Still, her heart soared at his words. He really liked her and was not put off by her body.

He dropped a kiss on her forehead and added with a wink, "For a virgin, you're a very good kisser."

She laughed and slapped him playfully on his shoulder.

"So, do you have a boyfriend?"

She smiled as thoughts of Mezie came floating back into her head. It no longer hurt like before. "I used to. I imagined we would get married and have children, but it didn't work out that way."

"What happened?"

She shrugged. "Feminism happened. He said it was ungodly."

Eric's raised eyebrow made her remark, "I know, right?"

He understood her passion for women's rights and her wish that more men would stand with them. Like always, she wished the circumstances were different for them. This man truly understood her.

"He also probably got tired of waiting for our wedding night and is presently married to my neighbour, whom he impregnated before marriage."

"Your neighbour? His tone sounded unbelieving. "I'm sorry, but your ex is petty. No decent woman deserves that kind of blatant disrespect."

She didn't reply. The memory of his betrayal didn't hurt anymore. However, she was grateful when Eric switched the conversation.

"Compared to the leader of The Black Mamba, The Boss is a saint. He cares for his workers' welfare, but the only thing he'll never forgive is betrayal. On the other hand, Mr. Kolawole Amoo, the leader of the Black Mamba, is a psychotic mess"

"Who are the Black Mamba?"

"They run an organization like ours, too, but are more deadly. You're in charge of annihilating their leader tomorrow."

A huge weight of fear settled in Odion's stomach, and she began to tremble.

Unaware of her discomfort, Eric continued, "His members walk around him on eggshells because he can kill them at his whim. His organization also engages in sex trafficking, which I find difficult to stomach. Speaking of stomachs, his couriers still carry cocaine inside their bodies, and we both know the implication of that."

She nodded to show that she understood. One of her mother's brother had died from cocaine bursting in his stomach. "How do you guys transport yours?"

"We make use of materials."

"What kind of materials?"

He smiled at her in the way her pastor did when he had to put up with her questions before answering, "Foodstuff and others. You'll get to know about them as time goes on."

She nodded. Then, a thought hit her.

"Omigosh! Like those yams I saw in that room?"

He regarded her keenly for a minute as though wrestling with inner thoughts before saying, "What you saw were not really yams but containers made to look like them."

"What? Those were not yams?"

He shook his head. "At all"

Odion shook her head in wonder. "Wow! You guys are really good."

Eric simply shrugged in response.

They sat in companionable silence for a while. He broke it first.

"Listen, Odion, there is an ongoing rumour about Mr. Kola's fetish with the knife during sex. The sorry part is that no woman who has ever been with Kola Amoo has lived to tell the story or confirm the rumour. Still, there is an element of truth to every strong rumour." He seized her hands as a frantic look stole into his eyes. "Promise me that when you find yourself alone with him, you'll shoot without hesitating if he ever picks up a knife."

Her brows furrowed as she tried to figure out his statement.

But he repeated, "Promise?"

"I promise," she replied, and his shoulders relaxed in visible relief

Rising to his feet, he stretched his hand to pull her up. "Come on, you are yet to give me a perfect shot."

***

The following morning, Odion received her briefing in the Boss' office. She would be driven to Eko Hotel and Suites where she was to somehow magically attract the Black Mamba leader, have him take her to his bed, give The Boss' message, and then kill him afterwards.

Hearing the Boss say it made it look so easy, but it wouldn't be. Still, she couldn't do anything about it. The life of her mother was at stake. She refused to let her mind dwell on the fact that she would be spilling the blood of another human on this day. Instead, she plotted and strategized on how she would carry out the act. It helped to keep her mind busy.

Soon enough, she arrived at the hotel, and the driver dropped her off at the entrance to the Reception. He would wait in the car park until she gave him a call. Asking the receptionist for directions to the lounge, she ordered a glass of Chapman after settling in and waited for her prey.

***

Odion waited 'til midday before she noticed a stir of activities. She didn't need any soothsayer to tell her this was Kolawole Amoo when he walked into the lounge. Even if he had come without his bodyguards, she would still have known.

Power screamed from every pore of his skin, but nothing had prepared her for the sight of him. The man was tall and dark-complexioned, with very handsome features. He could have been a modern day version of Adonis if not for his eyes—cold and lifeless, they made her recoil with fear.

Her mother had once told her it was easy to read a man through his eyes, and she could see that for herself now. His eyes announced that he had no soul, and instant fear gripped her. *How she would execute this job for The Boss?*

Nevertheless, her work had to be done, and she tried in vain to steal his attention obviously on somebody else. Then, he beckoned to the lady. *Oh, no.* If she didn't act fast, her mother would be in grave danger.

As his lady interest passed by her, she put out a foot to trip her, causing the woman to fall flat on her face. She, on the other hand, finally got what she wanted: Kolawole Amoo's attention. She gave him a big smile and held her breath while he seemingly hesitated. Then, he nodded her over. Her heart and head sang beautifully in sync. *Finally, step one.*

Odion straightened her gown, patted her afro wig, and walked towards Kolawole. It was now or never.

CHAPTER THIRTEEN

Odion Osahon

Mr. Kolawole's laugh rang out loudly through the lounge, which pleased her a little. She had always been teased about being an I-too-know in her neighbourhood, but today, those little titbits of information she had gathered on different subjects had come in handy. The man actually seemed to be enjoying her company, swirling a glass of brandy.

"Do you watch football?" he asked.

She gave a genuine smile. She loved football. "From time to time."

"And which club would be your favourite?"

"Liverpool."

Surprise formed on his brows. She was used to that response.

"Liverpool?"

"Oh, yes, Liverpool. We never walk alone."

The man laughed again, and it grated her insides. She didn't like the way he laughed or the fact that he was laughing at her choice of club. People tended to underrate Liverpool, and she didn't like it.

She watched him struggle to rein his laughter.

"Why Liverpool, of all clubs?" he then asked.

"What's wrong with Liverpool? Yeah, we may not have won the Premiership for a while now, but—"

"Did you just say a while?"

She could see another round of laughter building up and quickly added, "At least, we can boast of the UEFA Champions League cup."

"True." He nodded.

She raised an eyebrow. "I'm assuming you're with Chelsea."

He gasped in surprise. "How did you guess?"

She simply shrugged and rolled her eyes. "You guys are always cocky."

A lot of Yoruba guys she knew were Chelsea fans, and on some days, she actually wondered if it was a tribal thing.

He grinned, and she smiled in return.

Her eyes caught someone, and she froze. Was that—

"A penny for your thoughts?" Mr. Kolawole cut in.

She shook her head and smiled. Tension was making her mind run riot. She still had not figured out how she would shoot this man. In the lounge or his bedroom? Which would prove dangerous? On top of all that worry, she was now seeing things and people who were not supposed to be here in the first place.

One of his men approached their table.

"Yes, Saheed."

Saheed bent down to whisper in Mr. Kolawole's ear. "One of the key men from The Eye is here, sir."

Key men? Saheed's whisper had been loud, and she'd had no trouble hearing what he had to say.

Mr. Kolawole asked in his normal tone, "Where is he?"

"At the corner to the right."

Odion looked across the room with them and gasped. Eric. *What was he doing here?*

"Ahh, I see." Mr. Kolawole's smile looked deadly. "So, Brian Francis chooses to send his nephew instead of messengers, for a change."

His face turned serious and deadlier. "Get the men ready. We'll be sending Brian Francis a nice present."

CHAPTER FOURTEEN

Eric Francis

Wearing dark sunglasses, Eric sat at the corner of the lounge in Eko Hotel with a lady in front of him for company. He had invited her over to his table solely for the purpose of acting as his shield unbeknownst to her.

Observing Odion from his corner while listening half-heartedly to what his companion was saying, he could admit she was definitely handling this job like a pro. You would think she had done it before. He hoped she would be able to follow through with her assignment. A big, burly waiter brought drinks to his table.

As he took a look at the drinks, his guard came up. "This isn't what I ordered."

The waiter bent to place the drinks and spoke in a low voice meant for his ears only. "There's a note for you on the tray. It's urgent."

Eric picked up the note and read, '*Get out now. It's a trap.*'

He placed it in his pocket, and the waiter had barely left when three well-built men in black suits walked to his table purposefully.

"Our boss requires your presence," one of them said.

"Who's your boss?"

"Mr. Kolawole Amoo," another replied.

"I see." Eric remained surprisingly calm. "Where am I supposed to meet him?"

"Outside."

"Okay."

He stood up and excused himself from his female companion and set off a cacophony of confusion.

CHAPTER FIFTEEN

Odion Osahon
Eric is the Boss' nephew?

Why hadn't he said something? Saying she was shocked to see him would only be putting it mildly. For a minute, she had been rendered dumbfounded. Mr. Kolawole also noticed because he threw his head in Eric's direction and asked with narrowed eyes, "Do you know that man?"

Think fast, girl. This man is as smart as they come.

"He looks like one of the clients that frequents my office."

"Oh, okay." His shoulders visibly relaxed as he nodded.

She exhaled slowly. Obviously, she had said the right thing.

One minute, she saw Eric walking ahead of Mr. Kolawole's goons, and the next, he had stumbled, seized one of the men, and shot the other two. It all happened so fast and seemed like a flick of his wrist.

Mr. Kolawole pulled out his gun and shot at Eric who used the third goon as his body shield. The poor guy was repeatedly sprayed with bullets while Kolawole took cover from Eric's bullet spray with one of the tables.

Men of the Black Mamba, all dressed in black, poured into the room in large numbers, and just when she thought Eric was done for, the men of The Eye organization announced their presence with a loud roar as they rushed in, shooting. Even the Boss had come with them.

This was the first time she, Odion Osahon, would see people being killed at close range and bodies dropping to the floor like toothpicks. The gory sight of it all chased away the little courage she had built up before now. She had grown beyond terrified. People were ducking and running helter-skelter, and she joined them. This would be a good time to escape.

***

Odion was close to the hotel entrance when she stopped in her tracks. Where was she running to? She would not be safe no matter where she went. She would only be endangering her life and her mother's, too.

What should she do? Talk about being caught between the desert and the Red Sea. Best she turned back and hid somewhere. If the Black Mambas won this battle, she could slip out and escape. But if The Eye won ...

She sighed. "The devil you know ..."

The police siren approached from a distance, and she hissed. Even the police could not be trusted.

CHAPTER SIXTEEN

Agnes Osahon

In another seedy part of town, Agnes Osahon paced the threadbare carpet of her living room, deeply biting her lip without feeling. She had a strong foreboding that something terrible was happening, and this troubled her spirit. Despite her daughter's disappearance, she had never doubted that the girl was alive ... until now. She decided to do what she knew best in situations like this. She decided to pray.

"Heavenly Father, You are and will always be the great and mighty God. Only You can do what no one can do. Take charge of the life of your daughter, Odion, whom You entrusted into my hands twenty-five years ago. I have played my part accordingly and taught her Your ways. Now, her life is in danger. I can feel it.

"O, Daddy, You are the only one who can save her. I know everything happens for a reason. Manifest thy power and give us a testimony that will cause tongues to wag. Remove Odion from the jaws of death and bring her home safely. I plead with thee, o Lord, believing in my heart that You have heard and will answer. I am forever grateful in the name of Jesus Christ. Amen."

She stood still. Over the years, she had learnt to wait after saying her prayers instead of rushing off. Confirmation would always come. It could be anything from a scripture verse, a word, or a general sense of peace.

And as she stood alone in her dingy two-room apartment with furniture that had seen better days, a sense of peace enveloped her entire being.

Her shoulders relaxed visibly, and she heard a clear voice whisper, "Be still and know that I am God."

CHAPTER SEVENTEEN

Odion Osahon

Two things registered with Odion the moment she arrived at the scene of conflict. The Boss lay helplessly across the floor, unarmed, and Mr. Kolawole had his gun pinned on Eric's temple.

She sucked in her breath, her thoughts scattering in different directions. Palpitating fear gripped her heart, and she took off her afro wig, removing her gun hidden there. She filled the chamber all while muttering prayers for Eric.

Kolawole Amoo still had his back to her, standing close to the entrance. As she drew closer to him with stealth, he barked out to the gang members of The Eye,

"Drop your guns and kick them towards me."

The men looked confused in their move to comply, and she knew there was no more time to waste. Quickly, she placed the muzzle of her gun at the back of his head and cried, "Drop your weapon."

Kolawole Amoo froze. A heady sense of power filled her, and she clicked on the catch of her gun. Immediately, the leader of the Black Mamba raised his hands in surrender, and Eric promptly snatched the gun off his hands.

A victorious smile hung on Eric's lips now, and he gave her an almost imperceptible nod. Her insides began to tremble as she proceeded with the words which The Boss had made her memorise.

"Take this message to the grave. I am your messenger of death."

Before she could pull the trigger, another gun was pressed against the back of her head.

The male voice screamed, "Drop your guns, or I'll blow her brains out."

"Don't shoot, don't shoot!" Eric screamed and hurriedly moved to comply.

She did not know what came over her afterwards. Maybe it had been bravery or mere stupidity as she placed a well-aimed elbow on the side of the man holding her hostage, causing him to clutch his ribs in the process. It was a defence trick she had picked up from the streets of Oshodi.

She did not know what happened after that. A volley of gun shots rang from all sides, and she dropped to the ground as well as Mr. Kolawole.

CHAPTER EIGHTEEN

Eric Francis

The waiter who had given Eric the warning note earlier stood smiling with hot smoke emanating from the semi-automatic rifle in his hands.

Eric was even more surprised to see the Boss, his uncle, hug the man and say, "Tony, I knew I could count you," with a joyous chuckle laced with relief.

Eric's eyes swung suspiciously between them. "Do you know him?"

"From way back," his uncle replied excitedly. "I've known him since my youthful days."

He nodded without saying anything more and stared at Kolawole, their legs almost touching. His blood was collecting on the shiny marble floor, and his immobile hands could no longer gather them, lifeless just like his eyes.

Something kept nudging him. Then, it came.

"I thought your Lydia said he could only be killed by a virgin," he threw angrily at his uncle.

"Obviously, she lied," came the grim reply. "She has some explaining to do."

Eric was no longer listening. His eyes had fallen on the object of his unconscious search, and an agonized scream tore out of his throat, "Odion!"

CHAPTER NINETEEN

Odion Osahon
She locked up her office and dropped the keys into her bag, delighted to hear the jingles as it collided with her car key. She could never get tired of the sound. Choosing to walk today instead of drive, she briskly headed for home during the ten-minute walk, savouring the evening air as it blew gently against her skin.

An immediate difference could be felt even in the air when she stepped through the gates of the estate. Rows of neat hedges lined the streets beside clean gutters covered with slabs. The tarred roads and silent streets reminded her of her blessings, and she sent a prayer of thanks up to Heaven once again. This place existed worlds away from the rowdy streets she had grown up in. The approaching sight of brown, uniformed buildings gave her some sort of comfort. Among them lay her own flat—*their* own flat.

This is Home.
The preacher often said that good things came out of bad situations, and though she tried not to dwell on the source of her money, the honest truth remained that money from The Eye had transformed their lives.

After gaining consciousness from the shock of her close shave with death, Eric had insisted right there and then on her release and even pushed for her payment when the Boss had finally agreed to his demand. Though the Boss stubbornly argued that Kolawole Amoo had not died by her hands, he'd finally yielded to Eric's insistence and paid a lump sum as her compensation package.

Eric had been an angel through it all, her angel. He was the reason she'd relocated to Abuja, bought a place for herself and her mum, and started a large format print company. For a nine-month-old company, it was doing quite well.

A lot had happened after her departure from Lagos, and Eric had kept her informed. They'd discovered Lydia was a mole from the Black Mamba, but she had shot herself in the head before being captured. A gang war had developed between the two rival gangs, and news on TV and media outlets reported of war between cultists and bloodshed.

If only they knew the truth. She was simply glad she no longer resided there.

Voices drifted through the open door of their flat. Mum was always leaving the door open even with the A/C running. She sighed. Some habits were difficult to change. Her thoughts came back to Eric. They were always about Eric and his kind eyes, finely sculpted body, arms toned for a woman's loving touch, his—

She shook her head. She could not continue torturing herself like this. It had been six months since she'd heard from him, and still, his thoughts plagued her sleep and waking reality. Had she made a mistake? Should she have stayed? Would she have been happier in that world? She shook her head. She couldn't have. The Bible taught her not to be unequally yoked with unbelievers. Yet, she wished they had met under different circumstances. If only …

No, she shook her head. Best he kept his distance. She needed to get a grip on her new life and move on. Still, her resolve twisted her insides like a knife. What if something had happened to him? She had no form of contact with him. He had always called with a private number.

Standing at the threshold, she was shocked to see her mother's visitor.

Eric.

"What are you doing here? You never called or told me you were coming!" she asked as she stepped into the sitting room.

He shrugged uncomfortably.

"I wanted to be sure," he replied with a smile.

"Sure of what?"

Now, she was beginning to get angry. All that endless worry for nothing?

His eyes beseeched her. "Why don't you sit down first and hear what I have to say?"

Her mother chose that moment to exit the room. *Traitor.*

She complied. The moment she did, he stood up and began to pace the sitting room, clearly looking unsure of himself. She had never seen him this uncomfortable before.

When he met her eyes again, she smiled sweetly at him and mockingly said, "So, I get to sit and you get to stand?

"Come on, Odion." He was smiling now, clearly exasperated with her. "Haaa." He shook his head. "This woman!"

"What's wrong with 'this' woman?"

"She's the woman I want to spend the rest of my life with."

Odion felt the room tilt, her insides beginning to bubble. *It couldn't be.*

"What are you saying?"

Eric walked to her and bent to her level, holding her hand. "It just was not the same after you left. I didn't feel my old passion or enjoy the job. My uncle noticed it and asked me to contact you. In his words, 'get laid' and then come back. The moment he mentioned it, I realised that I didn't want to come back. I wanted to make a life with you."

Tears filled her eyes as he continued.

"I wanted a life of peace just like I enjoyed as a young boy before my parents were killed." His voice cracked, and he swallowed.

Her heart felt his pain, and she understood. "I'm sorry."

He nodded. "My uncle brought the wrath of a rival mafia gang to my family's doorstep." A faraway look crept into his eyes and he continued tonelessly. "They were his kryptonite, and their death would devastate him. It's the way of our world." He then paused, looking directly into her eyes. She saw his pain and the memory of it. "My parents were murdered in cold blood, and I watched from the hole of the cupboard I hid in."

She held him in a tight embrace, willing his pain to disappear through the warmth of her arms.

"I can't continue to live in fear of having a family of my own." He spoke firmly, with conviction. "I can't give my parents' murderers victory. They don't own or control my life. I do! I would rather spend the rest of my life happy rather than empty and safe. You're the woman for me. The one I want. Marry me, Odion."

She put up an offended look. "I can't marry you just because you want me."

A smile curved his lips, dousing his tenseness and at that moment, he looked beautiful. "You want me to use the L word, don't you?"

"Of course, yes. In fact, you should even get comfortable with it because Christians use it a lot. Christ loves the church, and we must love one another."

Eric laughed out long and unhindered, a tinkling sound that suffused warmth and a whisper of tomorrow into their lives and their world.

"It's time I came back to the church. I love you, Odion Osahon. I loved you from the moment our eyes met in that forest."

She pulled back a bit and looked into his eyes. "And from the time our paths crossed, our hearts decided our fates. I love you, too, Eric Francis."

"I love you even more."

"Well," she grinned, "I don't mind you winning in that area."

As he crushed her in his embrace, she closed her eyes and raised her lips to his, sealing their promise and future in a kiss as old as time.

The birds out there were flying and chattering noisily in the blue, wide sky, collectively travelling to their various nests.

She had found her home.

ABOUT THE AUTHOR

Julie Onoh is a Nigerian writer and poet whose love for books stemmed from her early childhood. So, it came as no surprise to her family and friends when she began to create her own stories and poetry. A firm believer that writers can make a positive difference in the world through words, she loves happy endings and is passionate about the welfare of the girl child. You can find her works in the Poetry Marathon Anthology (2019), The Kalahari Review, Ink Sword Magazine, Blaud Magazine and a host of other projects.

Connect with Julie on Instagram:
https://www.instagram.com/julieonohwrites/

Julie Onoh

Temenos
OBINNA OBIOMA

TEMENOS by Obinna Obioma

A bloodthirsty assassin on the loose, a website that cannot be hacked, and double locks on every door.

DSS Agent Lisa's primary objective is to find the vigilante behind the ritualistic murders. But her quest to unmask the evasive enemy might cost her everything including the love of her life.

CHAPTER ONE

That Saturday morning, the sun had burst forth earlier than it should, but it hid behind a foggy Harmattan cloud, unwilling to behold some murderous plot thought through the night. Just a few persons graced the St. Thomas Catholic parish by this time, sinners in need of Father Edmund's ablutionary grace. By seven-thirty a.m., the confessionals would be over, and the priest would be ready to retire to the vestry.

Ericson 'Eric' Kamalu had chosen this specific time to lay waste the wanton priest, his erstwhile counsellor, through a clean shot to his balding head—a smooth transition to Purgatory where, if lucky, he should be able to repeal his middle-aged soul from the fiery damnation of Hell.

"One blessed bullet." Eric kissed the .38 Smith & Wesson he'd always had, bought from a gun dealer in the black market. He blinked, his eyes scratchy and hurting as he tucked the gun behind his back, away from prying eyes.

He'd left the house and had barely walked to his parking lot when two police vans screeched into the terrazzo-ed compound. Three uniformed men in their deep shades of black, armed with assault rifles, jumped down from the tailboard of a Hilux 4x4 where they'd been perched.

Eric stood rooted in his spot upon noting that these were not ordinary mobile policemen. These came directly from the *Department*. These were *trouble*.

Three crestfallen Catholic nuns in their white and blue apparels emerged from the other van, took a glance at him, and whispered conspiratorially to another female in mufti who had a DSS badge dangling from her neck.

In a moment, the young woman, probably in her early thirties, beckoned to two of the rear guards and walked over to him.

"Good morning. Ericson Kamalu, I presume? Agent Lisa Rafferty," the slender-framed, athletic-built detective said as introduction.

She looked pretty—average height, chocolate-brown skin—but she struck him as the kind of lady who walked about and worked in unisex clothes, having no care for fashion. Her face said this was the usual broaching parlance, and Eric was in no mood for felicitations, either.

"What is going on here, Agent?" He gestured to the home invaders now strolling about his premises, unchecked.

"How long have you known Father Edmund?" She fixed him with cold eyes.

He frowned. "As long as he's been priest in my parish."

"And you were with him yesterday, yes?"

Eric was now very aghast. "Why do I think I need a lawyer, Agent?"

"Father Edmund was found murdered in his office a little while after you drove out of the parish—"

"Wait! Hold up!" he interrupted. "What does this have to do with me?"

He could ask nothing else when the profundity of the demise of the very man he'd wanted to murder came as a hard purchase.

"Were you with the priest yesterday?"

It seemed Lisa had decided to play hardball, her gaze narrowed as if in impatience while she awaited the indicting confession which she probably thought wittingly or unwittingly would come now.

"I was with the priest yester— No, I was *supposed* to be with him, but I never went in to see him," he stuttered. "I didn't kill him, if that's what all these seem to imply," he protested.

His had just been a murderous thought. Someone, obviously, had beaten him to his game, and for that, he would be eternally grateful. For now, he tried desperately to exonerate himself from the very complicated fix he'd found himself in.

"Unless everyone who'd come to see the Father for counsel yesterday is culpable here, then I am not," he tried vehemently again.

Surely, whoever had seen his face to recognize him must have seen the face of every other person, his whoring *fiancée* included.

Yesterday, after working hours, he had gone for his usual marriage counsel session with the priest. This, in accordance to church doctrine, would hold for a week, after which he would tie the nuptial cord with his fiancée, Samantha. They had agreed to meet at the Cathedral and then drive home together after the session with Father Edmund, but she had not been about the premises when Eric had gotten to the rendezvous point a little after four p.m.

As he'd taken the last flight of stairs into the vestibule that held the priest's office, something had caught his attention, causing him to demur on his path. The sinfonietta of 'Hail Judea' had aired andante from somewhere behind the vestibule— surely the choir at practice, it being Friday. But he thought he'd heard something else, a sound that did not belong.

He'd listened closely, deadening his ears to the cascade of the orchestra and at the same time listening above it.

Again.

It had come from along the hallway through to the church offices. A stifled scuffle, screech of wooden desk; a few second later, frantic slapping sound of maybe sweat-embossed flesh, then a deep guttural groan.

Eric had wondered what atrocities belied the inner veils of Father Edmund's chamber, as he'd been sure the sensual sounds emanated from within. Sensual, intense, and rough—like starvation fed by desperation, he'd thought, and a devilish grin had pursed his lips.

The priest was human; God's acolyte, but fickle still. Even clerics proved vulnerable to such arousing allurements the fair daughters of men have in their employ to lure mundane men out of their wits!

He'd decided to let the busy priest be. Of course, if the priest was able to absolve men of their guilt, he should be able to do the same for himself now he'd fallen away, had still been falling away as the moaning struggle had intensified from within, and the intermittent scraping protests of the office desk could still be heard. Even to the heights of sin, he'd been sure the Father, sworn to a celibate life, could redeem his soul.

His heart gleefully alight, Eric had turned to go. He'd decided to call Samantha to cancel their meeting with the priest. But the phone had rung aloud from the hallway a few paces behind and kept on increasing. He had frozen on his path, the naughty smile vanishing from his face, smothered with a grim perplexity as he'd listened to the familiar Safari ringtone of his soon-to-be-wife's cell phone air from the priest's office?

He'd dialled again. Seconds later, his surety had come, unanswered. It was his fiancée's cell!

"What in the heavens!" had been the words repeatedly torn from his throat as a thousand premonitory questions had jumbled his senses, almost benumbed by the shocking possibility that his bride-to-be was having an affair with his church priest!

Oh, Sam.

How he *had* loved her. Once, he'd rescued her from mortifying dishonour, saved her from the shackles of self-abasement inadvertently caused upon by the miscreants of society. He'd loved her and told her to breathe and live, even though the very air she had to breathe was polluted with the vileness of men's guile.

Three years was not a long time to forget, was it? Eric had decided he must save his face and hers from this eternal shame before they made a bigger mess by walking down the aisle. It was the only way.

But judgment had to be passed on Father Edmund. The priest was way over his head in sin, found wanting in three out of the six commandments that affected men—Eric had added stealing. Nothing but the blood of the priest himself could absolve him of this guilt and quench the thirst of vengeance that had dried Eric's lids and heart. How would the Father ever even stand to wed them? *No sin, no cross. No blood, no forgiveness ...*

"I'm sorry, Mr. Ericson." The detective's voice brought him back from his distant thoughts. "The closed-circuit TV footage placed you around the office section exactly at the same hour one of the nuns testified you went in to see the priest— his only visitor for the day after confessionals ..."

Eric's head reeled in a thousand direction as the detective explained away. *Who* had been with the Father in his office when he'd come around? And now, there were CCTVs in the house of God? The cams should have placed Samantha at the scene, too, for he had heard her phone ring from within, twice!

Or had he not? What fortuitous coincidence had he been made to face in the strained heat of yesterday? He'd been filled with every punch and peep and disdain and then a seething apathy when Samantha had come back later in the evening to confess she'd had her hands full in the market and could not pick his calls ...

"Sir, if you would please come with us for further interrogations," the detective said cautiously. "This is a formal arrest, and you have a right to a federal attorney—"

It happened so fast. Eric, quick as lightning, pushed her away and drew his gun. How was he to be convicted for another's crime all because a camera had caught him entering and leaving the dead priest's office section within same hour he was found dead by an aged nun who could as well be lying?

"Suspect is armed and dangerous!"

"Suspect is armed and dangerous!"

The warning rent the air as everybody dove for cover, and Eric fled up the stairs into his house. But he was not fast enough. Bullets riddled his back before he'd made it to the door.

A horrified Samantha heard the splitting gunshots and came out to see her husband-to-be crumpled in a heap on the front porch, bleeding, dying. She cradled him in her arms and wept bitterly.

CHAPTER TWO

Few years later ...

DSS Agent Lisa Rafferty was hoping for a break when her partner Abdul waltzed into her office. One look at his excited countenance, and she knew a case, direr than could be thought, had come up.

"You might want to see this." He slid a newspaper across the Formica table.

Lisa wordlessly picked it up.

"What the—" she gasped when her eyes had scanned the length of the columns.

While the Department fought to close cases, somebody was playing Grim Reaper, nailing the souls of men. The paper held the most bloodied content she had ever seen in her entire career. Two flagellated bodies scourged by Hell's own tongs, with phalluses clipped and stuffed into their mouths, etched with same message on their left thighs.

She broke out in sweat despite the air-conditioning. This was not the work of a psychopathic serial killer. No—a bloody assassin with a message: *TEMENOS: REAL MEN DON'T RAPE,* had made itself known. The words had been tattooed into the victims' flesh with a crude instrument used inexpertly.

She was suddenly not entirely sure where else she had seen a parody of such a gruesome scene.

"You might want to check out this *temenos.*"

Abdul's advice jolted her from the grisly reverie.

Minutes later, she sat over a whirring system, musing over the red marquee streaming along under the website's name and spider logo.

"Welcome to TEMENOS: The Sacred Circle where you can be yourself without fear."

Black *Latrodectus sp.* crawled protectively over the graphic display wherein a column expressed the objective of the organization in bloodcurdling terms: *"To every rapist in the country, if your number is up, we will find you!"*

"Jesus Christ! This is a cult!" She looked up at Abdul.

He shook his head. "It is worse. It's an organized online syndicate with strong and secured connections, where rape victims mete the *deserved* justice to their assailants through a faceless agent. Anonymously, that is, and at a price."

Lisa gazed at her system again. "Justice, you say? They leave no web signature?"

"None. And Intercom said the site was launched a few hours before the combo murder. Few hours! And TEMENOS has test-run its program to show the public it meant business!" Abdul shrilled.

"No." She thought differently. "It meant revolution."

CHAPTER THREE

A bare-chested Viktor Rafferty lounged out the evening on the sun-kissed balconette downstairs, stretched out on the chaise longue. A bottle of beer, half drunk, sat idly on a small side stool in a pool of its own latent sweat. Two more, emptied of their content, laid on the floor. He whistled gaily to the tune of 'Radioactive' whose metallic sounds emanated from a stereo inside the house, so loud it drowned out every other hum of life that existed on the long stretch of Victoria Estate this side of old Ikeja.

With Imagine Dragons booming in the background, the ebriety of chilled beer, and a warm, worriless evening air-tagging along to both music and liquor, he eased out of this world to another where he hadn't heard his wife's Toyota Corolla cruise into the plot of their one-storeyed flat.

"And what is Intercom's whiz kid doing disturbing the entire neighbourhood when the rest of the world is on fire?"

Viktor's eyes snapped open at the sound of Lisa's voice, a smile gracing his face. Her shoulders hung limply, and he could tell she was helplessly tired. She'd started to pit out her favourite mufti.

"And what is DSS' sweetest detective *doing* smelling of musk, sweat, and shame?" he returned sheepishly, knowing the only fires he saw lay in the disapproval in his wife's eyes. Lisa hated loud music. And she hated that he'd decided to spend his entire leave playing housekeeping.

"Come inside, Viktor Rafferty. We're at world's end."

She rolled her eyes and walked into the house when his second trial at getting up failed.

"Detective," he called tauntingly after her. "A local drunk of a husband needs a hand out of a chair! And a hug, too!"

He caught up with her clambering up the stairs leading to their bedroom after he'd turned down the volume on the stereo.

"Hey, Mona Lisa," he teased, spun her around by the elbow, and kissed off her tiredness. He was used to this staircase egg treatment, the usual on days she came back wearing the weight of the world's problems on her neck.

***

His mouth lingered, his tongue searching, and Lisa wanted to savour every arc of the moment, wanted the straying hand now cupping and caressing her breasts to stay, wanted to hang onto the masculine essences of alcohol and a higher sex drive. The underlying desperation of his arousal poked through his track pants and hit her hip.

The rhythm of his throbbing heart aligned almost synchronous to hers, but her heart pulsated for far more foreboding reasons as the gory images and wordings she'd seen earlier in the newspaper played out in her head, striking her with a soul-wrenching illness she thought she'd outgrown. She dreaded the invading feelings so much that she unwillingly broke off the amorous entanglement.

Viktor's brow wrinkled with concern. "Baby, are you alright?"

"Yeah, yeah."

Her response definitely lacked the needed assurance, but she didn't want him to worry too much about what she'd been through today.

"You should have seen how clueless they all looked today," she said with a tinge of truthfulness.

"Who?"

"Your boys at Intercom."

"*Ow-kay.*" Viktor's face relaxed at the likely promise of a good gossip from work. "We'll talk over dinner, then. Your boy cooked." He winked conspiratorially. "You go freshen up."

He then ran down the stairs towards the kitchen.

"Oh, good son of Malik ..." Lisa smiled faintly. She appreciated how Viktor came in handy in the kitchen during his leave days, and he always got his extra bout of *bed work*—'recompense for filling in for you during your excusable absences from *your* culinary duties,' he always said. She wondered if she'd be able to make love tonight, talk less pay her *bills* in bed; not with this new gossip tugging her heartstrings.

Viktor hemmed and hawed during the entire meal while Lisa's spoon played peek-a-boo with the grains of jollof rice never meeting her mouth as she prattled on about the combo murder cases and the launch of a daredevil web site that had never been heard of.

"Whoever would come up with such a murderous plot?" she asked.

"One that has a personal vendetta with rapists. And the high tech touch to it? Blow me!" Viktor munched in excitement.

"Oh, Viktor Rafferty, be serious. No one pops out of the blues and decide to cleanse the street of rapists!"

"Except a hurting fellow."

She ignored his assertion and continued. "I won't be an advocate of jungle justice. Come to think of the calamity that will befall mankind if every aggrieved person is allowed the *will* and technology to take law into their hands."

"Says the one who's never felt the pains of the abused whose cases are stowed away and the culprits merely walk free, unscathed."

Viktor's candid concern touched her, but it hurt that he'd pitched her to a safe side—the one protected by the law. She did not blame his misgivings, for she'd never told him anything about her grim experiences. She felt safer with them stashed in the dim and distant past where they belonged.

Finally, the spoon finding her mouth, she asked, "How can such a site be hacked?"

Viktor started to rattle in turn. "Or infiltrated, yes? Well, err ... We could flood the site with a DOS or DDOS. This should stop the functioning of the web system by sending a couple thousands of fake requests to the server's request queue. When this happens—"

"Alright, alright, whiz kid. Leave's over. You need to get to work, ASAP." She caught him off, picking his empty dish and hers, half-eaten, and headed to the kitchen.

"Is this not the part where I get a 'I'll meet you in the bedroom later', babe?" he chimed after her.

"No. This is the part where I dump these plates in the pantry, hit the bed, and go right off to sleep—to think in my dreams because I'm dead tired to do so in reality!"

CHAPTER FOUR

In a few days, TEMENOS had been flooded with hundreds of membership log-in and sign-ups. In a week, thousands—and none of these was Viktor's own making. It kept growing and spreading like an aggrieved disease. The whispers were true. Some 'vigilante' had called out every rapist in the state and beyond to duel. Within months, the populace was caught in #PIM #RMDR hash-tag frenzy. With every bagged body, the blogs spread like wildfire in the Harmattan wind.

A Facebook and Twitter platform existed— a closed group where members shared experiences and expectations. And both were hitting a million-plus followers. Raped and sexually abused victims had finally found their safe haven, where they could share their experiences anonymously, meet people of like mind, and pass judgments on their abusers.

Viktor was not surprised some victims wanted their abductors to face such inhumane execution as the faceless vigilante passed on the culprits. They only had to click to buy a 'bounty' of 100,000 points.

First, they funded their TEMENOS e-wallet with their cash accounts using their banks after a biometric registration. Next, an invoice was generated for the contract, where the 'abductor' ID and photo got uploaded through a redirected channel.

The client would then 'appeal' to TEMENOS, and 100,000 points would be withdrawn. When the transaction had been confirmed, the member received the 'RAPE' tool, an acronym for *Rapid Abductee Protection and Emasculator*. The rape tool marked the timer when the client waited a period of fourteen Internet days during which 'the body drops'.

And for the gutsy, pained, and rich, half a million bucks in national currency was not hard to pay to request for the blood of the one—or ones—who'd caused them such trauma as they'd experienced in the never-forgotten past.

To the lily-livered, TEMENOS tweeted: *'Revenge or Forgive'*.

And to the entire men of the Department, whose lawful duty meant stopping TEMENOS, it said: *'Justice is fair when justice is extreme.'*

For eleven months, the Department remained clueless. His wife had been assigned to the case, and for the first time, she was helpless. All attempts to hack TEMENOS proved futile. It protected its members' profiles and clients, and at the same time, it merged with the crowd. Its e-wallet accounts proved untraceable, sourced to a foreign crypto account.

Unidentified, untraceable, faceless— TEMENOS worked in the shadows. Viktor helplessly watched a social media that raged on with a trend of vengeance and an obsessed Lisa pitched at the forefront of those inexorably chasing after the wind.

The Department had to make do with counting body bags and answering to unrelenting, story-thirsty journalists who carried what gory tales and bizarre graphic content they could find at any crime scene to their frightened viewers.

But to the enchanted TEMENOS faithful, every *'the Department has again failed to apprehend the vigilante who still is at large'*, which concluded the correspondence during the 9PM National News, was always received in felicity ...

CHAPTER FIVE

"Baby, could you turn off the television and come to bed?"

Viktor's voice startled Lisa. She'd not heard him walk into the sitting room. She glanced at the wall clock—10:15 p.m.—and the ticking told her she needed a good rest. And more, her husband needed her, too.

His need for her grew against her thigh when he pulled her up from the couch and planted a sensuous kiss on her lips. Warm, imploring, but not enough arousal for a distracted Lisa whose eyes still darted to the screen where another 'temenos' breaking news made the headlines.

"Baby, I need you," he whispered desperately, sucking in air dense with her perfumed hair cream when he nuzzled close and held her lush hair to his face.

"I know, honey, I know," she whined helplessly when his teasing tongue again left her lips, and her hands, which ordinarily should have continued playing with his muscular biceps and shoulders, fell frigidly to her side.

"Honey, I-I can't concentrate. Can we try again much later?"

His face fell. "It's the case, isn't it?"

Her frustrated eyes held her unspoken plea.

"Baby, you can't keep allowing your work get between us. It's been so long since we had a good time," he iterated. "A real good time."

She sighed and looked to her cold feet for help. TEMENOS was not just stealing the souls of men; it had deprived her of a normal love life since she'd been assigned to the case. She pitied her husband and wished he could understand that everything that transpired seemed connected to her unforgettable past.

Each time the vigilante struck, her past called to her, loudly, urging her to find the balance where her judgments would outweigh the scales of justice. But no! It was her life that got weighed down.

If only Viktor knew how badly she wanted him, too, desired a long session of sweaty, 'screamy' lovemaking, like it once had been. If only he knew that the shrewd imageries of her past still played out in her head each moment she wanted to soar in his arms. If only he could feel the cold emanations these thoughts brought with them.

Two nights ago, they had tried, but it had not been satisfactory. As Viktor had pounded away, she'd relived the numerous moments in the past before she met Viktor when 'the squirrel' had forced himself on her. She thought she saw the grim visage of her sole adversary in her husband's face …

The sound of Viktor's footfalls, stomping away in dejection and defeat, brought her back to the present. As she stared at him dragging his feet up the stairs, she hoped this would not be the last straw that would break the camel's back.

CHAPTER SIX

Viktor sat alone in a computer lab somewhere in the heart of town, lost to time. The room looked like another digital world of computer systems: littered wiring and interconnections, electronic blips of a couple of wireless devices, and a potpourri of computer technology, all fashioned into one hermetic private lair. The supercomputer sat before him, having the famous friendly Mac interface, and another PC simulated numbers and program codes that ran through the screen in colour shades of red, blue, and green.

Another beep made him glance at his tablet. Yet another *'please come back home'* text from Lisa. The sixtieth message or so—he'd lost count—since he'd left home. For what he'd set out to do, he could not go home, not until the TEMENOS mystery had been resolved. No, not until he could look into Lisa's face again and see no hint of worry.

She was right. No clime was safe from the vengeful demon that even threatened to put down men of the law. It grew stronger with each spilled blood—the vigilante needed to be checked.

Last week, a commissioner of state had been taken down in his hotel, amidst all his security detail! How? No bullet hole. He was discovered dead— strangled and emasculated. It had been a big hit last week, the biggest hit since this year of the macabre saga.

The bodies dropped anywhere: homes, hotels. One was done in his car, as if the Angel of Death had reached out and stopped his clock before the brute did his ritual.

At a time when the world thought the devil played by no rules, a female body 'dropped' for the first time, with a tweet: *'TEMENOS is for the sexually abused, not for infidels.'*

They said someone had tried to book a bounty when the target had only been a political rival and no rapist. It had boomeranged. TEMENOS had dropped the girl whose biometrics had been used in trying to lure it into the political assassination. Nobody could tell how it found out. They said the demon could smell the guilt of its targets from a distance.

And so, the DSS stood with their hands tied, lacking in ways to lure it out without having to endanger the lives of their agents.

Deciding to take the bull by the horn, Viktor put in his resignation from Intercom Inc. and disappeared into reclusive days, bent on luring the vigilante out with the only bait he had. *Himself.*

CHAPTER SEVEN

Lisa rose from her bed. With restless ears and a caffeinated mind, she could not sleep. Not with the haunting nightmares and aloneness which greeted her days. She reached for the lights and walked drowsily to the closet which had been improvised as her private lair for the *temenos* case.

The plywood wall held a large map of the country littered with red dots of needle heads. Thin threads of ribbon joined these dots in pattern-less recurrences. That was how the *Shadow*—as she had nicknamed it—worked: in no definite pattern. It struck anywhere it found its victims. Ten out of seventeen had been maimed within the cities of Lagos. Seventeen souls sent to Hell, and still counting!

No gender specificity could be pinpointed for the Shadow yet. Many thought the vigilante to be an aggrieved female, who'd resurrected from the cocoon whence she had been plunged into by some ghastly rape incident, bringing retribution to her adversaries and suchlike.

But the strength, swiftness, and ferocity with which the Shadow carried out its judgments defied such any known woman could bring about. And hence, a greater percentage thought him a man, ex-military, come to redeem the helpless and effeminate. Others just thought *it* to be some angel or demon, calling it the Scourge of God.

Lisa sighed.

Every serial killer she'd come across had a pattern that would eventually lead her to him or to their next victim. But this ... this was no serial killer. This was a hired gun, but with a crude, diabolical method, drawing out every execution as though it were a ritual. One for all within the 'sacred circle' where its followers were safe.

She thought about the many times she'd wanted to be 'safe', feel *that* protected and safe. Once at thirteen and then at fifteen, she'd been helpless when they'd all happened ...

She edged out of the claustrophobic closet into the bedroom and caught her reflection in the mirror. In eleven months, she'd lost a few pounds chasing after someone who had the guts—and wits!—to do what she'd always wished to do but could not within the premise of the law.

She had lost Viktor, too. He'd complained she was obsessed with her work, the TEMENOS case. He'd said he would come back after a few days; said he needed time to think their four-year-old marriage through. It had been three months now since Viktor had gone away ...

First, it had been frustration, then obsession. Now, she was depressed.

"Darn the law!" She kicked the bed, which squeaked its innocence. She'd joined the Department to put bad guys—such as the Shadow—behind bars. Only, her job involved not just nailing rapists, but criminals, the lot of them!

But then, justice had never been fair. Was it not two years ago a serial rapist had been let off the law's hook because the dad was a senator and the mother a commissioner of state? And, oh, after much tweaking and weighing of the weights between 'intent' and 'consent', those who made it to prison walked free after a few months, and the abused, traumatized souls were left to languish in psychological peril forever.

"Darn the Department's crackpot vision!" she cursed into the night.

It was the first time she'd spoken against the department she'd sworn to uphold and serve.

Okay. Not the first time.

Three years ago, a suspect had been shot when he'd been making a safe and *unthreatening* retreat into his house. She still recalled his name. Ericson. He'd been armed and running; never a threat. But Sala and Rico had shot him point blank in the back! Who shot a suspect when he was making an escape into his own home, surrounded?

The man's fiancée, Samantha, she'd cried crimson. Her boyfriend had been guilty to an unproved extent, she'd admitted, but he had rights. She'd taken up her case up with the Department, and they had allowed it to slide.

Lisa had protested that the officers face tribunal and the woman be paid full recompense for her fiancé's death. She'd been slammed for standing up for a murderer.

A murderer, they'd called him. Without trial!

Ericson would have faced a minimum jail term for unlawful possession of firearm, if he had proven his case. There'd been no fingerprints; only the footage, not of the murder, but it would have been enough to put the man away for a time. But not for life, and certainly not for dead!

The Department had seen a murderer; Lisa had seen a confused, frightened man with a gun. *Whatever was he doing with a gun?*

But Father Edmund had not been shot. He'd been strangled, his genitals cut off and stuffed into his mouth ...

Wait a minute.

Lisa suddenly rushed back into the closet with the springiness of a cat. She opened the lower drawer on the chest and rummaged through case files until she found the three-year-old picture of the murdered Father Edmund in his office. She then crosschecked all the pictures of the Shadow's victims, starting from the first.

That!

The *Phallus-In-Mouth* insignia she'd first seen on the Shadow's debut execution earlier this year had first appeared three years ago ... *This* was the Shadow's method, but on a subtle note.

This could only mean ... Whoever had killed Father Edmund had not been the armed, frightened Ericson who'd probably happened to be at the right place but at a wrong time. They were dealing with a daredevil, a mastermind, someone able to evade hidden cams.

Jesus Christ! How long had the tree of liberty been irrigated with the blood of the innocent? Lisa slumped into the swivelling chair. A lot suddenly bore on her conscience. Her eyes fell on her idle laptop always logged to TEMENOS. The mystery behind the Shadow proved compounding, with Father Edmund obviously the principal quarry in the arbitrary blacklist. *Was the holy father a rapist, too?*

She could hear the cries of Ericson's fiancée louder now, crying for help from a not-too-distant past; the persistent nightmarish cry. She bit her lip.

Revenge or Forgive.

It was time to work. Not for the Department.

For Ericson Kamalu.

She must avenge him—Lisa swore inwardly, drew her laptop closer, and clicked on the sign-up icon …

CHAPTER EIGHT

Today marked the beginning of the twenty-one day TEMENOS Sabbath which would culminate into the New Year. During these weeks, there would be no executions. To declare the blood-free holiday open, TEMENOS had made a public release:

"The battle against sexual abuse is an unending one as long as there are frail feminine preys in our neighbourhood and heartless, hateful men to abuse and molest them at will. These are women, wives, daughters. Their predators: men, husbands, sons. These weaklings are your neighbours, food vendors, hawkers, maids— daughters of men. Look for them in your pasts. You owe them an apology."

Abdul rose gallantly from the leather upholstery when the DSS Director walked into the oval office through a door that connected the superior's office to the archives.

"As you were, Agent," the short, rotund man gesticulated. His voice rang heavy with the *Yoruba* accent as thick as the double-lined tribal marks etched on both sides of his cheek. He was a bland man in his mid-sixties, with unsmiling features, a perpetual soreness that Nature had deemed fit to bestow upon his person.

Maybe it was the 'seat', thought Abdul as the Director heaved into the big, black, leather swivelling chair. They said none who'd occupied *this* DSS seat at the helm of HQ in times past hadn't had anything to smile for.

Two years ago, when the Big Man—as he was popularly nicknamed—had ascended the throne, they said he'd done so with an oracular air. From Day One, he'd told anyone summoned into his office how their future with the Department looked. Some oldies, older than him, got retired, and the younger sluggards saw their asses set ablaze.

So this hot noon, when he was called into the Big Man's office, Abdul had his fears, and his sweaty brow showed his exasperation. He didn't have to wait long to know what the summoning was about, for the director was not one to waste precious time in trivial conversation, or so they said.

"Now, Agent Abdul, what do you think about that on the screen?" The Big Man gestured to the big flat television screen which displayed the Temenos Sabbath message.

"Sir?" Abdul was lost, put off by the unexpected informal air of his superior who rarely asked anybody what they thought. He was known to only give orders and counter orders.

He stared in discomfiture, not knowing what to answer or how exactly the director wanted him to *think*.

The Big Man gave a mirthless smile which died on his lips as soon as it formed. "Nobody knows anything. *Nobody* thinks anything. But if there is something I know, it is that we're dealing with an emotional, sympathetic vigilante who loves Christmas. This war will soon be over," he prophesied, "and you, Agent, might live to see the end of this tale."

He flashed a set of dentition—discoloured by tobacco and numerous lobes of kola—in an ominous smile that chilled the junior officer's blood.

Abdul made to speak, but the Big Man waved him off.

"Everyone is afraid whose head the guillotine might fall on next, but such like me whose hands are clean, well ..." He trailed off with a distant gaze, as if seeing past the mounted screen where his eyes had been glued to.

The junior officer was not at ease with the director's diffidence. Whatever issue it was, the Big Man sounded prophetically mysterious, and the suspense did Abdul's mood no good, either.

"You're being reassigned, Agent Abdul." The Big Man finally dropped the bombshell, rubbing his small pudgy palms together and jabbing into Abdul's straying thoughts.

"And my partner?" Abdul spoke for the second time in a sweaty half hour despite the humming air-conditioning.

The Big Man smiled wryly and looked down to fix his gaze on him. "She is your new mission."

CHAPTER NINE

The nation was in tumult. During the wee hours of the New Year, at the expiration of the Sabbath, TEMENOS had tweeted its New Year's resolution: *"They thought to traumatize your future. Dig up the cesspit of their past to heap on their present graves!"*

By morning, men flooded the DSS Precincts in fright, requesting to be jailed for rape which they had committed years ago or in recent times.

At the Department's HQ in the Federal Capital Territory, hundreds of men banged at their barricaded gates, seeking entrance and refuge into their cells, running from their guilty consciences and the threatening surge of the unseen.

"Anything but the Scourge of God," they cried.

Those who'd heeded the Sabbath command overtly had called out their one-time victims on the social plugs and begged for their forgiveness, knowing their lives' worth hung only by a hundred thousand points. The *Temenos* price might seem unattainable to the poor, but not to the resolute hell-bent on revenge.

Meanwhile, the revolting girls were nowhere to be seen. In the mixed multitude of the TEMENOS convent, they were the everyday faces of sunshine and rain, gathering points by the hundreds to get even with their past, in sworn anonymity.

Viktor was watching the ongoing protest on the national news from a plasma screen when he heard a knock on the front door. After a minute's rummage, he retrieved a 9mm revolver from a crowded drawer filled with nameless oddities and checked it for bullets. The oiled gun held behind his cotton shirt, he proceeded tentatively to the front door.

A peep through the security door hole, and he decided all was safe—a lady in red, looking harmless. He glanced at his watch. 6:15 p.m. Probably one of the very few callers who found themselves lost in this lonely part of the town.

The door opened with a metal screech, and he stared into the face of the unfamiliar caller only to be greeted by an absorbing and totally disarming smile.

"Hi, Viktor?"

"Yes?"

He didn't have time to wonder. It happened so fast, he didn't have the time to think what struck him. His entire neural system immobilized at once when the stun gun sent ripples of electroshock coursing through his body.

Crumpled to the ground before he blacked out, he could only see the blurry form of the woman hover about him and think how his plans had worked all too soon and how he'd failed Lisa ...

CHAPTER TEN

It was a calm neighbourhood, rich and lush in structures, reserved for the rich and holding the most expensive plots and houses on this side of the island. No concrete fencing except that which enclosed the entire estate to be seen here. Painted palisades demarcated each plot from the other, just high enough to check domestic pets.

From her vantage position—the last floor of the spa, in the hotel where she'd lodged—Lisa had kept watch over the lemon-green house for a week. When she was not at the spa, she sat amongst the clusters of pine woods, still on the opposite side of the avenue, sometimes watching into the middle of the night. The *squirrel* never left its hole.

Safely hidden between the pines, she had no fears of being seen. This neighbourhood rarely thrived with people. Only a few passers-by and more cruisers-by in their tinted cars who had no business with whatever happened by the side of the boulevards graced Banana Estate. So she had almost an entire avenue as her hideout, blending in when the esplanade got a little busy.

At high noon, mother and daughter came out of the house with some light luggage, accompanied by a man who posed as a father figure. They hurriedly drove away, without as much a word or show of affection to him. He indeed had a squirrelly disposition, restive face, and squinty eyes that said he could not be trusted. *Age has not changed him one bit*, she thought.

He withdrew back into his hole after seeing the duo off to the bougainvillea strip that bordered the front stairs. Fear had made him paranoid; never exceeding the interlocked walkway where he felt he might be an easy mark.

Today, the seventh day of the watch, Lisa could feel the man's fears in more ways than he could, even as the shadows loomed over the duplex with the setting sun. So caught up was she in waiting than when death came for the Squirrel, she did not see it drive past her into the plot.

It was a fair beauty, dressed in red apparel, the very colour of seduction: slender, supple, with a cleavage that would make one drool in admiration of her south-eastern charm.

When *she* stepped away from the black, sleek Lexus SUV in long stilettoed strides towards the house, she looked every perfect inch of a young Marina mistress, but not a killer. Not until she Taser-ed the Squirrel at the door, mechanically catching him mid-air and dragging him into the house, in a sleight of hand that confounded Lisa—one the man didn't see coming.

Lisa's eyes widened with recognition, and heat flushed her face in clear surprise when the *mistress* turned to close the door behind her.

It was *her*! The Shadow! Lisa knew instantly. She was the one who'd fetched the wormy wood. Now, the lizard had come to feast.

A few minutes later, the seductress came out of the house and went to the trunk of the vehicle, dragged down a struggling man in fetters, and lumbered him into the house.

Viktor! The recognition hit Lisa with a stomach-wrenching nausea and fear.

"Oh, Viktor, Viktor! What have you done, you stiff-necked fool?" the now distraught agent cursed and cried, before reaching desperately into her jacket for both badge and gun.

CHAPTER ELEVEN

When Viktor came to, his hands were bound, and he'd been dumped in a corner of a well-furnished bedroom. He still felt the volts of stunning energy from the zapping shock he'd received. The groans of a man called his attention to another captive, laid supine, naked and gagged, strapped to a table in the middle of the bedroom.

The man tried his waning strength at tugging at the strap; useless, though. Bound with wire gauzes, he only ended up twisting bare flesh. Blood trickled from his right thigh where the thin metallic strip drove into his skin the instant he put up a struggle. He whimpered in fright.

"It's alright to be afraid," came the voice of their captor; a hoarse, sorrow-stricken voice that trailed into an ominous whisper and sometimes rasped as a siren's call.

"Fear is the first instrument."

The clank of metals rattled as she laid out her crude implements of torture on the mirrored oak cabinet. Each item, she looked over, inspected lovingly, as though longingly admiring a newly acquired shiny gem. But time and use and blood had washed the metal lustre off the tongs and pincers and scissors and acupunctural needles and the chunks of ten iron branding letters.

And then, there was the big electrical device, the emasculator— the treasured tool of her devilry. She plugged in its cable to a power source, fingered the switch, and allowed it to hum loud and long until the buzzing sounds died out and nothing else could be heard save for the intermittent sniffs of the frightened man. She rubbed her black-gloved hands and grinned satisfactorily at the shiny steel blades of the hedge clippers.

The man moaned and kicked like a helpless rat caught in a trap when she came, looming over him. But she ignored him and looked in Viktor's direction. Her eyes appeared stony, a kaleidoscope of black, grey, and gloom; the very opposite of what he'd seen the split second before he'd been Taser-ed out cold.

The stun gun—that's how the vigilante did it. Element of surprise. *She* just walked into your life with a Taser. You don't see her coming; you don't know your number is up. And the fact that it *was* a woman still filled him with awe and now ... respect. His only regret was he would descend to his grave without confession, and the world would never know TEMENOS was no more a mystery.

Viktor's heart ached at the thought of Lisa. If only he could see her again, be given the chance to reveal everything to her ...

"How could you be so stupid, geek?" The voice of TEMENOS—now in flesh—cold and piercing, jerked him out of his improbable wishes. "Do you think *I* was not protected against your SQL injection attacks?"

The tech pro found his guts and voice. "Yes, of course, I knew you would be."

He noted the glint of self-adoration that brightened her visage when she talked about TEMENOS in the first person. *When God is a woman* ... he thought to himself.

"What?" She frowned, stepping away from the whimpering man whose face was already bedewed with tears.

"I said, humans, we've all got our vulnerabilities. I tried to find yours."

"Hmph! Leaving a dent of your malicious virus tracing back to your download source and address?"

Viktor smiled mirthlessly. "Yes, because I wanted *you* to find me."

The smirk turned into a deeper scowl on her mascara-ed face.

"You brought your death upon yourself."

She then turned away to glare at the man below whose face had become a pool of hot tears streaming down his cheeks, his nose running shamelessly.

"It's alright to be afraid, Mr. Nathan Ake," she said again to him, a false note of consolation in her voice. "*She* was afraid when you went into her, the searing pintle of your masculinity forcefully taking her innocence from her. You gifted her *early* tears and drew pleasure from her pain. You tore her heart when you tore the fleshly veil and drained her future's life of blood. This is your just comeuppance, Mr. Ake."

She brandished the emasculator, and that concluded the perfunctory death speech.

Tears shimmered in her eyes, too. These moments broke her, and there had been twenty-four of such— not counting the infidel— during the calendar year. This would be the twenty-fifth taste of vengeance when she would feel the spasms of her afflictions afresh, when she would watch him die in her arms again ...

"How old was Anita Yakubu when you destroyed her?" she asked the weeping Ake now looking very aged in fright.

He struggled with the woollen gag, eyes almost bulging out of their sockets. She pulled down the gag to free his mouth.

Ake croaked finally when he found his breath. "It's not Ani ... whoever you called. It was *Lisa*. Lisa Rafferty! And she was thirteen!"

Viktor's mouth dropped agape on hearing the man's confession.

Almost immediately, a loud bang sent splinters of wood flying as the bedroom's door came apart!

CHAPTER TWELVE

"Samantha, drop the scissors," Lisa pleaded, gun clutched firmly in both palms and levelled at the woman.

Samantha edged the scissors threateningly to Ake's sweaty throat. The sharp edge tore into his skin and drew a trickle of blood.

"I'll slit his throat before you think to take me out," she hissed fiercely, squatting lower beside the table to hold firmly Ake's strangled neck.

Ake winced in pain.

"I don't care if he dies, Sam." Lisa shook her head. "But I care that you get out of here alive," she said meaningfully.

Ake's eyes flared as his hope of salvation waxed and waned with Lisa's noncommittal declaration. He stifled his protests and pleas.

"It's just you and me. We can work something out." Lisa put her palms up, then cautiously dropped her gun to the floor. Samantha's eyes followed her every movement.

A subtle kick, and the handgun slid across the marble floor to rest at Samantha's stilettoed feet. She let go of Ake, deftly picked up the gun, and levelled it at Lisa's head.

"I could kill you right now ... or him."

The gun now pointed to Viktor who huddled by the corner, still dumbfounded at the turn of event.

Lisa glanced at her husband and held his gaze. He was suffering, and for a dividing of time, she wished she could just smack his face for using himself as bait, then wrap warm, soothing arms around his shoulders and tell him that all will be all right.

She looked at their captor squarely in the eyes. "No, you won't. You won't kill an innocent man. That's not your MO."

A measured moment passed between them before she broke off the gaze and casually walked over to the table top cabinet to look over the tools of the Shadow's punition.

How crude and how ironical that most implements of female genital mutilation were used as instruments of men's torture, with an animalistic bonus. Her eyes drooped at the *sadcasms* and suffering her kind had been made to face for far too long. Sufferings she'd endured when she was still in her prime. Her gaze drifted to fall on the king-sized bed to her right. It held a lot of memories, sad and indecent. The entire house did. She glanced at whimpering Ake, her chest tightened with rage.

Samantha's hands slacked and fell to her side, as if tired of holding out the weight of death to one who posed no more threat to her, even more overturned by the melancholy which suddenly had enshrouded Lisa's visage. Somehow, it was as if she saw her reflection in Lisa—a woman of sorrow, now almost in league with the dark.

"You knew I'd figure out your ploy if you'd used your real name, Agent Lisa?"

Lisa smiled wryly.

"Somehow, I had to outwit you. Sent a single 'fake request'—" she glanced at Viktor. "—the DOS plan, recall?" She then shifted her gaze to Samantha. "I fed you the quarry you needed."

And then, finally, it came to rest on Ake. "I gave you my sorry story, my dark past, *him*."

Samantha nodded. There was always that risk in belief, when it was more-than-a-head knowledge. This was another mistake; just like the first time ... She hoped the consequences wouldn't be as fatal.

"I know you killed the priest, but I never suspected it would be *you*. Not in a million guesses." Lisa looked up at Samantha.

"That mongrel! He shouldn't be called a priest!"

Lisa's mouth twitched, and her jaw tightened as her eyes urged Samantha to spill.

Samantha paused for a moment, as if considering if she should let the agent into her woes. Then, it seemed she finally deciding to pour out her heart. "I was only fourteen, the little plantain-chips hawker of Bariga, and he was in the seminary ... He spent the vacation with his uncle who lived in our neighbourhood. I always sold to him ... until that deserted noon when he invited me into the house for my money ..."

She could not continue as she broke down crying. She could almost see him, feel him defile her little innocence. An unwary little chick, she'd strayed into oblivion. She was little, but she'd learnt shame from society, to know shame when she experienced shame. And so ashamed was she that she grew afraid to confide in anyone after it happened. If he could stifle her protests and cries, pound her tiny waist for two minutes which spanned into eternity, and then tell her to dry her tears and clean her bloodstained skirt, what other consolation could the world give? That noon, she'd tried to walk her usual rounds, but her shadow had limped. And the unbearable pain between her legs— that had been her rite of passage into obscurity, until Ericson Kamalu came into her life.

Lisa walked up and pulled the crying demoness into a close embrace. She felt cold and frail as she sobbed violently, allowing all the tremors and pains and fears of the past to gush into this one moment of weakness. You'd hardly think this poor crying thing was capable of anything ... of repossession—taking back from *everyone* who took from her.

"It's alright, Sam," she consoled.

"I couldn't watch the very man who tore me into shreds stand at the altar and wed us!" Samantha cried. "He took my life. Eric gave it back to me. Eric didn't deserve to die!"

Lisa didn't know why she could no more see the rotund Squirrel tied to the table, until the hot tears which blurred her vision streamlined her cheeks. She looked imploringly at Viktor who'd sat still, speechless, taking in what he could.

The moment of revelation. No escaping it now.

CHAPTER THIRTEEN

That squirrel of a man there *was* her stepfather; the curse of her childhood. When Father died, Mother had remarried. To Nathan Ake. Lisa had been barely thirteen when her mother died in a ghastly auto-crash. Then one night, drunken Ake had come back home, to this same house, and had pounced on her.

The pains of it, the scars, the torn dignity! And then, he'd threatened to kill her if she ever breathed a word about it to anyone. Was she not already dead? There was no one to tell, no schooling, no chance at telling when she was caged, imprisoned here, in this room, a little sex slave—torn and healed; broken and mended to be broken again.

More nights of horror, of creaking bed frames and stifled cries of anguish, of threats and growing fears counted by each fading moon, until she broke through her pains, broke a few windowpanes, and ran away from the nightmarish Marina duplex ...

At fifteen, could it be freedom at last?

No. It had been Lisa against the world and against the night muggers of Carter Bridge who'd taxed her body most nights in her little garbage-ridden space under the bridge.

One night, they'd left her for dead after a gangbang, but she'd crawled out and away from Hell until she was picked up by a couple who'd nearly run her over atop the bridge— Mr. and Mrs. Malik Rafferty, Viktor's parents of blessed memories. They'd been her kind foster parents who'd given her another chance at life. And Lisa had lived.

Where Viktor sat watching the parley, he could not help the tears that threateningly stung his eyes seeking for release. Father had never told him the circumstances behind Lisa's adoption. He'd flown in from Canada when Mother had died of cancer to meet the pretty, introverted damsel, and he'd taken an instant liking to her.

Almost within same age bracket, they'd gone on to grow up together. But it was obvious during his university days, when he'd taken up to study Computer Engineering and Lisa had been enrolled in the police academy, that they were doing more than just growing up together. And Mr. Malik had approved of it until his passing five years ago.

CHAPTER FOURTEEN

Samantha had stopped crying, drained of every fight and energy, purged of every ounce of anger and pain. Two years, she'd wept for Eric. Two years, she'd taken up military training, and twelve moons later, she'd gone AWOL to fight for him, watched men struggle in death in her gloved hands, thinking she would find relief, recompense, in each blood she drew with the hot branding tools. But nothing surpassed the calm she felt just leaning on Lisa's shoulder, listening to her tell her a story of a stronger woman.

Lisa was another Samantha story, but she'd come out stronger ... all by herself, and had risen to become another bounty hunter but this time with a badge.

Lisa was *strength*. And long had Samantha longed for a stronger shoulder—like Eric's—to lean the weight of her burden. Long had she wanted to unmask the faceless demon she'd become who carried out other victims' vengeance, to tear off the mask and weep herself to such calmness as she felt now.

She pulled away from Lisa's embrace and glanced at the whimpering unfinished business, the table's captive.

"I'm done," she said. "I'm shutting down TEMENOS. You can bring me in, Agent Lisa. I'm ready to join Eric."

Lisa thought for a moment, nodded stiffly.

"Yeah. I'm done, too. I'm done chasing you. I wanted to avenge Eric ... I think I have now." She looked into Samantha's blurry eyes. "You can live your life for Eric now, Sam. Get away, far from here. If I could catch you, the Department someday will."

Samantha could not believe her ears. "I murdered a lot—"

"No, Sam. You executed. They were deserving of death! Jungle justice, yes, but I think we've lived our separate lives as shadows of ourselves. It's time to come out of it. I can't lose you, too, Sam. You must leave to live."

Samantha blinked furtively, fighting back fresh tears which sought to overpower her lids once more. She had her life back now. Once, she'd wanted to go on killing and killing, even if it was for the right purpose, until she was killed.

"How about him?" She jerked her head towards Ake.

"Don't worry. He's a relic of my past. I'll take care of him."

"Thank you for finding me, Lisa. For saving me … for this moment."

Lisa nodded and smiled wanly.

"Thank you." Samantha nodded slightly to Viktor, now unbound.

They were about to hug themselves *goodbye* when heavily armed and booted men stomped into the room. Troopers from the Department! Abdul had led the Crack Squad to Ake's home, and nobody had heard them come in.

"Abdul! No!" Lisa shouted, stepping protectively in front of Samantha.

"Step away from her, Lisa," he warned.

"No!"

For the first time, Samantha was afraid of the muzzles of guns staring her in the face, afraid of death. She huddled behind her guardian shielding her away from the gunnery menace.

"I tracked you here, partner. Was hot on your trail. Knew you would be onto the Shadow somehow." Abdul did a double take when he spotted the scourging tools on the cabinet and tightened his grip on his Uzi. "Damn it, Lisa! I was right."

"I am bringing her in, Abdul. Now stand down!" Lisa barked.

"No, you aren't."

Rico. He'd taken off his visored helmet.

Sala stepped forward, too, doing the same. "You are feasting with the she-devil, Lisa! Shame on you!"

Samantha suddenly felt hurt and enraged. She recognized the two agents who'd shot Eric and gone scot-free. Again, she felt the coldness of death clutched firmly in her palms ...

"I do this for Eric," she whispered to Lisa and quickly pushed her away from the line of fire.

"No!" Viktor's voice rose above the tension.

Two ear-splitting shots rang out— two agents dropped with a bullet each to the head— followed in quick succession by the splattering spray of automatic Uzi fire.

CHAPTER FIFTEEN

Newsmen and reporters were having a field day with the growing news, and the National dailies didn't have enough columns to write on their very exciting, sometimes hyperbolic headlines:

TEMENOS Vigilante Shot By Men Of The Department.
Two Officers Dead: TEMENOS Program Shuts Down.
The Invincible and Invisible Exterminated In Gun Clash.
TEMENOS Dies With Female Vigilante.
Faceless TEMENOS Agent Revealed.
Man Blacklisted For Execution Saved By DSS.

Pictures of the *Black Widow* who for twelve months had held the country's rapists in fear, for the first time, were released to the gaping wondrous view of the mesmerized masses. The TEMENOS faithful now saw their leader for what she *really* was—an ordinary woman.

Nathan Ake walked free as they could pin nothing on him after he'd played the abducted victim. For three weeks, Viktor Rafferty was held in custody. For his and Lisa's freedom, he brokered a deal with the DSS who carted away all the computers and accessories at his private digital lab and made him give up the program model he'd created to infiltrate and track TEMENOS.

CHAPTER SIXTEEN

Lisa sat, swivelling idly on the chair, staring at the laptop but unseeing the icons on the display screen; unhearing the intermittent beeping of the discharging UPS which begged to be plugged to a power source; unfeeling the droplets of sweat trickling down her brows; unheeding the cramps of her muscles, tired from sitting in the claustrophobic lair all day.

Lisa Rafferty had been dismissed from the Department and had barely been let off the hook on technical grounds after being tried by the Tribunal for oath breach, complicity, and dissimulation.

Three weeks in reclusion, she battled the dreadful uncertainty surrounding Viktor's arrest and mourned for Samantha. Samantha had stood up to the world, made it aware that rapists deserved punishment—something equivalent to what they made their victims pass through, something thorough, something capital.

And the many inspired girls now tweeting their revolutionary piece about rape on the Internet? Samantha had shown them they could outlive the dreariness and the effeminacy that men took advantage of. She'd taught them that men could be held to ransom, too, should they overstep their bounds. She'd carved them a niche where they would not always be afraid of their own weaknesses.

She'd taught Lisa that the likes of Nathan Ake did not deserve to breathe the cheery air of Mother Nature's goodwill.

Deep down, Lisa fumed, her breaths coming in short raspy succession. Something boiled within that needed venting.

She bent down and withdrew a flash drive from the lower drawer, read the imprint 'ROF'. Samantha had slipped it into her pocket before she'd pushed her down and away from the line of fire.

She knew what it was.

The key to *Hades* ...

The doorbell rang twice, startling her. She quickly mopped her wet face with the back of her hands.

Who could it be?

She was not expecting anybody in her lone world. The DSS still held Viktor in custody, 'for debriefing,' they'd said. Maybe Abdul, her erstwhile partner, had come to apologize, or it could be Ike, the laundry man who surely would come to return serviced dresses she definitely missed from her wardrobe but could not recall when she'd sent them to him.

Who cares about dresses and fashion, anyway? She scoffed. For all she cared, she could go on looking all unkempt and drab, as untidy and unwashed as the marble of the stairs she reluctantly clambered down. She paced through the dusty sitting room to the front door.

If it happened to be Abdul, she would talk him off and then bang the oak door into his face. And then, she would do something about her grumbling stomach which now protested against the inhumanely prolonged hunger strike, vehemently saying: *"let thy eyes and nostrils and heart mourn thy loss, but leave me belly out of thy depression."*

She peeped through the door hole, and immediately, her muscles tensed with surprise. It was Viktor! Calm as ever and in his disarming patient posture, he leaned against the rails of the front porch's balcony.

Lisa's heart raced. She could not believe her eyes. Her breath came in a short, ragged pulse, and—God!—it had the foul tidings of a whole day's shut-and-unwashed mouth!

Her hubby stood on the porch, and suddenly, all she could do was break out in sweat, dithering by the front door in confused perplexity even though all her heart had ever yearned for these past months had been to be in his arms again.

She ran her palms through the ruffled strands of her hair. *No, God! Not when I'm a picture of the word 'turnoff'.* She started to worry about her whole facial disposition. *When was the last time I ever had to worry about my looks?*

She made to run back upstairs, to seek quick magical transformation in the bathroom, but Viktor's baritone voice stopped her on her track.

"Baby, open up. I know you're in there."

Wide-eyed, she yanked the door open, and her husband's ravishing frame came into full view. His muscular chest seemed to rip apart the checkered cotton polo shirt he wore atop a pair of blue jeans. His eyes twinkled, irises as dark as his trimmed beard. He did not at all look like one who'd been through the hassles of DSS' interrogation! The entire corridor seeped with the scintillating fragrance of his *Smart* perfume—exotic, overpowering—and Lisa realized how much her olfactory nerves had missed the alluring scent of him.

"Hi," she exhaled uncomfortably, avoiding his misty eyes.

She did not know how he'd taken the fact that she'd not confided in him about her grim past when he'd been the major tool that'd shaped her life, giving it so much meaning and fun cached in her memories.

Viktor did not utter any word, but within the moment, covered the distance between them in three calculated strides, and the next thing Lisa felt was his arms wrapped around her in a close embrace.

"Vik—"

"*Shh*," he hushed her, squeezing her to him as her slender arms returned the hug, the tension about them both gradually lifting.

They nuzzled for a minute, hearts throbbing in rhythmic duet until they formed a drum line of one.

Lisa's eyes welled up with tears when Viktor angled for her lips.

"No, Vik, no," she protested.

"I know you smell horrible with grief, and I'm sorry. I'm sorry for everything that's happened to you. For running off to fight alone and causing you more worries and pain. Will you forgive me?"

She gave a teary chuckle before Viktor's mouth enveloped hers in a lingering kiss, and all else ceased to exist ...

CHAPTER SEVENTEEN

Half-naked and squeezed into the small space of the couch on which they'd made love—the long, exhilarating, sweaty, and 'screamy' sort she had always desired—Viktor played with Lisa's hair.

"Jeez!" he screamed when he did a double take after spotting his polo shirt hanging awkwardly on the idle ceiling fan. He pointed. "How did that get there?"

Their clothes had taken different strategic positions on the marble floor and furniture of the well-furnished sitting room, and when Lisa could not find her brassiere anywhere in sight, she laughed loud and long, the sonority of her voice rippling the quiet February noon until tears shimmered in her eyes again.

And then, the duo was silent again, speaking with their hearts and skin. They'd had a long talk earlier, and Viktor had made a surprising proposition: the resurrection of TEMENOS—same thoughts she'd struggled with since the past week.

When he asked for the second time, "Are you sure you're ready for this, ex-agent?" breaking the silence, Lisa did not wait long before she answered.

"Yes. As sure as I'm ready to make babies with you, honey."

Her eyes held a distant gaze, seeing past the decking, to the flash drive lying beside the laptop in her lair upstairs, their soon-to-be den ... The Department had taken everything from them, but they had everything they needed. Samantha had made sure of that.

Two weeks later, a man was discovered dead in a Marina home, phallus-in-mouth, and a garish engraving on his left thigh read, *Real Men Don't Rape.*

A few hours later, TEMENOS tweeted: *'Back From The Dead'*

ABOUT THE AUTHOR

Obioma Obinna Kelechi hails from Abia State, Nigeria. He is a passionate writer and social activist.

His short story, Òsú, was shortlisted for the K and L Prize for African Literature 2019, and appears in Histories of Yesterday Anthology.

TEMENOS is his debut LAP publication. He is also the writer of the paranormal novella 'She Called Him God' which appears in the Enchanted series with Love Africa Press.

His poetry 'And Soaring With Bards' first appeared in an online magazine, Active Muse's Vasant-Spring Anthology for 2019.

When he is not writing, he is busy surfing the net, or at the movies, or glaring at Chemical engineering books.

Connect with Obinna on Instagram:

https://www.instagram.com/kheloberyn/

Honour
KIRU TAYE

HONOUR by Kiru Taye

A selfless act costs Kane everything and earns him a prison sentence. A power show gains him freedom and entry into the Yadili underworld. Family, loyalty and honour are all within his grasp.

Including Sahara, the daughter of his boss, who reminds him of the love he lost and she's totally off limits. A forbidden desire could cost him everything again, including his life.

CHAPTER ONE

Footsteps thumped along the long, dark concrete corridor. Two uniformed guards flanked Kane Waziri as he walked towards the thick gray door at the end. Metals rattled, and the barriers slid apart. Bright light burst through the opening, almost blinding him.

Lifting his left hand to block the glare, he squinted and crossed the threshold. Another twenty steps took him past the gated razor-wire fence. The clanging barricade behind him announced 'freedom.'

He inhaled heated arid air and surveyed the area. Pebbles prodded the soles of his booted feet.

The prison stood at the end of a long, dusty, empty road. There was nothing but green shrubs, trees and grey earth as far as eyes could see.

He tugged at his collar, the black t-shirt clinging to clammy skin. The pair of navy denim made his skin itch, considering they hadn't been his usual daily attire for the past twenty-four months.

What now?

No taxi would materialise out of the dusty haze. He had nowhere to go even if he did get a ride out of this no-man's land. No family waited for his return. No friends to let him crash on their floors until he could find his feet.

No one.

At least in prison, he'd had company, a roof over his head and one meal a day in his belly. There had been some normalcy to the grim existence.

Still, he didn't look back at the dark structure he'd exited, never one to dwell on the past. There was only one way to go; forward and into an uncertain future.

He heaved a sigh and started walking.

In the distance, a cloud of dust billowed in his direction. A few seconds later a black vehicle screeched to a halt, metres away.

"Need a lift?" a male voice called out.

Kane ducked his head to stare at the man visible from the rolled-down front passenger window of the luxury SUV.

"Okey, what are you doing here?" he asked in a disbelieving voice.

His former cellmate grinned, flashing white teeth. "I wanted to surprise you. Get in."

Kane's mouth dropped open. He'd long resigned to not relying on anyone but himself. Certainly not ex-prison buddies.

In a post-second-civil-war Nigeria that had become gravely fractured along tribal lines and where allegiances were polarised in a North versus South divide, he had never referred to a southern as a 'friend'.

Not exactly true.

No. He wasn't about to bring 'the woman' into this.

This was about Okenna 'Okey' Odili, the nephew of one of the most influential kingpins south of Rivers Niger and Benue.

He'd saved the man's life once, and Kane considered his early release from prison sufficient payment for that favour.

The man owed him nothing, and they weren't friends.

Kane had no friends. He didn't need them.

He was a lone wolf.

Okey hadn't turned up here to give him a free ride out of the goodness of his heart. Something was up.

Regardless of his suspicions about Okey's motives, he would take the lift in a comfortable car rather than trek for miles fuelled by nothing but principles.

Principles were bullshit anyway. His had earned nothing but trouble so far.

"Thank you." He muttered and slid into the black leather back seat, pulling the door shut.

"The look on your face, though." Okey chuckled.

"I'm shocked. How did you know this was my release date?" Kane asked.

"I asked your lawyer."

"You mean *your lawyer*. You paid for him."

Kane couldn't have afforded the top tier advocate who had gotten his case reviewed, resulting in his prison sentence being commuted.

But with a cellmate like Okey, anything became possible.

"No more than his usual retainer. He's the family attorney. And after what you did for me, you are family." Okey tapped the driver's shoulder. "By the way, this is Nnamdi."

"Good to meet you," Kane said, meeting the man's curious gaze in the rear-view mirror.

"Same here," Nnamdi replied. His dreadlocked hair packed in a stylish top bun, he appeared younger in the button-up long-sleeve shirt, similar to his front passenger's. But while his was sky blue, Okey's was white with blue stripes. They both wore dark trousers. They looked like business execs.

This only reminded Kane of how out of place he was in the outfit he'd acquired from the prison store.

"Where to?" Nnamdi glanced at his front passenger.

"Back to the city," Okey replied and twisted in his seat to look back. "Unless you have somewhere else in mind."

Kane shrugged. "No."

He didn't know anyone in the state, and he wasn't in a hurry to go anywhere else. Right now, sitting in the comfort of the cool car rather than doing the long trek to civilisation under the hot sun was enough for him to relax.

Nnamdi spun the car around and headed away from the prison, stone crunching under the wheels, dust flying.

Another chapter of Kane's life was closed.

But was it?

Okey adjusted one of the knobs on the central diamond-cut controller disc, and Afrobeats filled the space. Radios had been luxury in prison, so the music sounded beautiful coming from the illuminated speakers on the door panels.

They drove for about two hours. Okey and Nnamdi occasionally spoke in Igbo. Kane didn't understand the language. But he could translate some essential words—something about a guy at the seaport customs.

He didn't blame them for excluding him when they talked business. He was little more than a stranger.

Which begged the question? Why had Okey turned up outside the prison today?

The music changed to a familiar up-tempo track. His heart battered his chest.

"Please increase the volume," he said before he could think better of it.

"Sure. You like the song?" Okey grinned as he turned the knob.

"I haven't heard it in a long time," he said.

Conversation receded, replaced by music. Kane was transported to another space and time.

Sitting on the bed and watching her sway to the rhythm of the song. He'd never been much of a dancer. But he'd been happy to watch her, every move, every smile, every curve, and every pore. Her hair messy and wild, as she smiled seductively, bewitching him. The time he'd spent with her had been the best of his life. Then everything had changed.

"What do you want to do first?" Okey's voice drew him back from his daydream.

Kane stared blankly at the man, working his brain to figure out what he'd missed.

The scenery outside the car had changed from brown arid rural grasslands through dense green vegetations to concrete, smog and city lights beckoned in the distance as the cloudy sky darkened to dusk.

"When I came out of jail, I wanted sex, sustenance and then sleep, in that order. What about you?" His prison mate continued and turned in his direction as the car joined the start-stop evening traffic across the business district.

Kane chuckled. "You did?"

Okey grinned. "Yeah, man. Three months in there was just too long to go without a babe. And you were in there a lot longer."

"True." Two years was a long time without the soft touch of a woman. A good night's sleep had been in short supply too. However, he craved something else. "I would really love some seafood okra soup."

"Sustenance, it is. I know where to get the best food in town."

CHAPTER TWO

Neither of the men exchanged words. It seemed Nnamdi knew where to go. Thirty minutes later, he pulled to a stop in the parking lot outside a two-level cream and blue building with 'Olivia Restaurant' sign over the fascia.

Kane got out of the car and paused to absorb his surroundings. Sounds of the city swarmed him—beeping car horns, pedestrian conversations and loud music from local shops.

Prison life hadn't exactly been quiet. But this was different. The vibrancy of life around him was overwhelming and exhilarating.

"Are you coming?" Okey stood at the entrance of the premises.

Kane joined him and nodded at the uniformed security man when he walked past. The packed restaurant reflected the energetic atmosphere he'd witnessed outside.

Okey didn't wait to be seated. He strode through the diner as if he owned it. Half of the guests greeted and shook hands with him, his cocky, flamboyant manner evident. Then he stopped at a round table with a 'reserved' card set for six and pulled out a chair.

Kane scalp prickled as he followed.

His former profession had involved wearing a uniform regularly, same as his time in jail. He liked blending in with his environment and not drawing attention to himself.

In here, he surely stood out like a red stain on a white sheet with his scruffy appearance.

He'd been expecting to buy food from a roadside buka, not a top nosh restaurant. Perhaps he should have requested for somewhere to shower and shave first. Not to mention that the cost of the meal would severely deplete the limited funds he'd earned while incarcerated. He would need to find a job soon.

Still, he kept a neutral expression and chose a seat with a panoramic view of the rest of the place. Unease heightened his watchfulness.

A waiter appeared. "Good evening, Mr Odili, Sirs. What can I get you?"

They ordered their meals. Kane opted for ground rice meal to go with seafood okra soup. The men asked for beers, he went for a cola drink instead. He and alcohol didn't mix well.

"Okey, most people here seem to know you by name. Do you own the place?" Kane asked after the waiter returned with their drinks.

It would explain why the man hadn't been challenged about the reserved table since he hadn't called the restaurant in advance, although he could have booked online or with an app.

"No. It's not like that. Olivia owns the place, but we have a stake in it. We loaned her the money to set it up and have an arrangement with her. I'll introduce you to her later."

Waiters arrived with trays of food moments later.

Kane washed his hands in one of the sinks strategically located for diners who preferred using their fingers to using cutlery.

"Talking about business," Okey said between mouthfuls. "I'd like you to help me with something."

There you go. Kane relaxed into the seat. He'd been hoping there was a way he could pay the man back for his generosity. He didn't like owing people. "Sure, I'm listening."

"There's a guy, Mr Suleiman, at the customs department who has been making it difficult for us to clear our imported goods for the past six months. He demands more than we pay anywhere else, which is crippling for us. We hope you can speak to him."

"You want me to just speak to him?" Kane raised his eyebrow. He wanted to understand his remit. In truth, he wasn't much of a talker. His skills lay in other areas.

"We're hoping he'll listen to you since you're both from the North and speak the same language. Ultimately he needs to be persuaded to work with us."

Persuasion was something Kane was adept in. In another life, he'd been part of a highly effective and deadly elite team whose job had been to convince citizens to desist from any anti-Government actions.

Since the war, divisions between northerners and southerners had deepened. The federal government had taken a dictatorial, hard-line approach. Many of his tribesmen were in charge of administrative positions across the country. So it wasn't surprising that the ones down here would make life difficult for locals.

It wasn't his headache. He'd sworn not to get involved or take sides in the past few years.

Still, it hadn't stopped him from helping Okey out during a prison fight. He'd taken sides then because he'd seen the unfairness of the situation. Five men to one had been an ambush and unjust. He'd had to even out the playing field. Not to mention that the attackers had invaded his domain and sanctuary—the prison library. He'd had to assert his authority.

And if the customs officer discriminated against Okey's business for no good reason then, it would be unjust too.

"Okay. I'll do it," he said.

"Great," Okey cheered, raising his glass. "We'll go and see him tomorrow."

Good news. Kane could clear his debt to the man and move on straight afterwards.

From his peripheral vision, he spotted new arrivals in the restaurant, a male and female couple.

Awareness prickled his nape, and he lifted his head.

Straightened shoulder-length hair styled in flicked layers, the woman wore a navy midi pencil skirt, a multi-coloured blouse with ruffled sleeves, stilettos and purse to match.

Recognition dawned. Kane's heart jolted and his skin temperature rose.

The face he could never forget—oval-shaped, copper-penny skin, button nose, brown eyes and bow lips.

Sahara Odili.

Five years. Five goddamned long years since he'd seen her.

His stomach did flip-flops and his mouth dried out. He grabbed his glass and gulped the fizzy drink.

He hadn't thought a simple glimpse of her would rattle him.

Worse the couple were headed in this direction.

Shit.

The moment he'd gotten into Okey's car he'd known there would be a likelihood of bumping into her.

Yet, seeing her again made him feel hot and cold.

She represented everything he'd lost, and everything he couldn't have.

Heaviness settled on his body.

"Okenna," the male new arrival said when he reached the table. He wore a pinstriped suit like an old-world investment banker. He had an air of arrogance, but without Okey's exuberance. "You're back."

"Yes, we got in about an hour ago. Kane, this is Rocha." Okey said as he stood.

"Welcome," Rocha said but didn't extend his hand for a shake.

Kane nodded. "Thank you."

Okey kissed the woman in the cheeks and pulled out a chair for her between him and Rocha. "And this is Sahara, my cousin."

The woman stared at Kane for a few heartbeats, before sitting. Her face stayed expressionless.

Did she recognise him?

His appearance had changed. Years ago he'd been clean-shaven and sported a number-one buzz cut on his head. In prison, he couldn't allow anyone to come near him with a sharp object. He'd grown out his hair and wore a beard.

Now he looked like a brute, although he'd never been a candidate for the gentleman of the year award.

Another point of conflict. He didn't want her to realise it was him who looked like a stray dog. Yet, a part of him yearned for her to look at him with the same wondrous fascination she'd exhibited years ago.

Whether she identified him this time or not, she didn't say anything to him, focusing her attention on the other men.

Okenna called the waiter. Rocha and Sahara ordered food and drinks.

Conversation flowed around him, some of it in Igbo, usually instigated by Rocha who also ignored him. Rocha kept his arm draped over Sahara's chair. She didn't seem to mind the intimacy implied by the action. Were the two of them dating?

Kane's appetite receded, and his stomach hardened. He couldn't sit here and watch them.

CHAPTER THREE

"I'm going outside for some fresh air." He pushed his seat back and pulled out some notes from his pocket to cover his meal.

Okey waved him away. "No. The meal is on me. When we finish here we'll go somewhere you'll be taken care of and can relax. We can't forget the rest of the things on the list."

Kane stood, more concerned with putting some distance between him and Sahara rather than any pleasurable activities Okey had in store for him.

He nodded at the other men and strode to the sink where he washed his hands. Then he headed out of the restaurant, through the car park and down to the pavement. He sucked in a long breath, welcoming the humid night air and the bustling city as a distraction from thinking.

A couple of buildings down, a wooden kiosk stood on the sidewalk with vaping stickers. He hadn't smoked in months. A cigarette was a poor substitute for what he needed. But beggars couldn't choose.

He walked to the stall and bought a starter kit. With his back against a brick fence, he raised the eCig against his mouth and took a slow, steady, gentle inhale.

White menthol mist swirled around him. After a second puff, his shoulders relaxed as the nicotine struck his system.

"What the hell are you doing here?"

He turned his head in the direction of the angry female voice.

Sahara stomped towards him, her stilettos clicking on the hard concrete.

So she remembered him, after all.

He ignored her and took another drag of nicotine vapour, trying to relax again.

"I'm talking to you, *Kane*," she said his name in a mocking tone.

He sighed. "I'm trying to smoke in peace."

Who was he kidding?

The few seconds of peace he'd experienced with the nicotine hit was lost.

Not with Sahara almost next to him.

How come she'd managed to blank him in the restaurant, and he couldn't shut down his responses to her presence?

His pulse rate went stratospheric, and his light-headedness was equivalent to floating in space.

She always could make him feel high and out of himself.

Even when she was mad at him.

Now his fingers itched with the need to touch her, to map out every dip and curve of her body wrapped in those fitted clothes.

Damn. She'd filled out in all the right places.

Arousal flared in his gut. Two steps forward and they would have body contact.

However, the look on her shadowed face said she would gut him with a knife rather than get down and dirty with him again.

"Smoke in peace? How did you worm your way into Okenna's graces? You know what? I don't care how you got here. Just leave and never come back."

He swallowed hard and lowered his head. His stomach hardened, and he resisted the urge to crumple from the hurt.

If he'd needed a reminder that she hated him, here it was.

He'd been injured by physical weapons. Yet none had hurt the way her words did.

He deserved her wrath and had been foolish to think that he'd served enough punishment for his sins.

He wasn't good enough for her.

Maybe he should walk away like she wanted.

Still, he'd made Okey a promise to help with the man at customs. He never reneged on a oath. So he was obligated to stay until he resolved the matter.

He took another drag and blew out a white cloud.

"I can't leave. I promised your cousin I would do something for him. After that ..." He shrugged.

"You can't leave? Okay. If you're not going to leave, then I'm going to tell him who you really are." She swivelled and headed back towards the restaurant.

"Wait!" he called out.

She didn't stop.

Shit. He couldn't let her do as she'd threatened. The consequences...

He pushed off the wall, hurried and reached for her. "I said, wait."

She shoved his chest. "I don't have to do anything you say."

He grabbed her arm and used her movement to pivot her against the wall. "Hear me out."

"Let go." she snarled, body tense,

Still, he felt her curves, her softness and his pulse thumped with the awareness of her.

"Are you sure you want to tell him my true identity? Hmmm?" He kept his voice low so the pedestrians walking past wouldn't overhear. "Because if you do, you're going to have to explain how you know me and your boyfriend is not going to be happy when he finds out the truth about us, is he?"

Her eyes widened before her forehead rumpled in a frown. "You know what? Fuck you, Kane."

"We've done that already, Sa." He lost the willingness to cajole when she didn't deny that Rocha was her boyfriend.

"Don't call me that." She shoved at his chest again.

He didn't budge. "You used to love it when I shortened your name."

"I hate it now. Just like I hate you." Her eyes caught a fiery glare.

For a moment, his heart constricted. He should sling the words back at her.

Wasn't she the reason, he had lost everything. Like a hurricane, she'd smashed through his world and turned it upside down.

But the constriction in his chest wouldn't let him speak.

She shoved him again, and he stumbled back.

She didn't look at him as she walked away.

Why did her venomous words hurt?

She never used to be so malicious. Although meek hadn't described her either. The woman he'd known had been mischievous, yes, but affectionate.

He scrubbed a hand over his face.

Perhaps he really should leave town.

Exhaling another sigh, he placed the eCig on his lips. He would do what he'd intended to do first. Smoke in peace. Then he would go inside and tell Okey he was leaving.

CHAPTER FOUR

Vape stick tucked into his front trouser pocket, he strode across the restaurant car park.

Sahara and Rocha stood beside a dark SUV. She slid into the back seat, her eyes shooting daggers at Kane. Rocha nodded in his direction.

Inside, Okey and Nnamdi were chatting with another man who excused himself when Kane returned.

"Okey, thanks for everything but I'm tired and I'm going to find a place to lay my head for the night," he said. He would still sort out the customs officer because he'd given his word. But he didn't have to hang with Okey and his crew to do it.

"Hey, don't worry about it." The man stood and put his hand on Kane's shoulder. "Remember I told you I'd take care of you."

"I know and thank you for your help. But I can find my way from here."

"Nonsense, man. I've got you covered. Come on."

Walking away from an Odili was easier said than done, it seemed. Kane's past experience with Sahara should be enough warning.

He stopped arguing, nodded and followed Okey out of the building.

They got back into the car. Twenty minutes later, they were outside a guest house. Nnamdi waited in the car.

"You'll get a good night sleep here," Okey said as he led the way to another building beside the hotel. "But first you need this."

He tapped on the black metal door before he was let in by a burly man.

They entered a dark foyer.

"Oga Okey, welcome," a woman greeted in a sultry tone.

"Rosa, this is my friend Kane," he said. "Take good care of him."

"Of course." Rosa turned the smile in Kane's direction. She had a pretty gap-toothed smile, but the heavy makeup and blonde wig did nothing for him. "Girls, come out here."

A column of girls sashayed into the foyer and lined up against the wall.

"Take your pick." Okey grinned, thumping his back. "You deserve a treat."

Kane swept his gaze over the women of various skin tones and shapes. They were mostly dressed in lingerie although some had miniskirts or shorts.

He hadn't been with anyone in over two years, and he'd dreamt about succumbing to the pleasures of love-making several times.

Now standing only feet away from a selection, he could only think of the one who wasn't here. The one who could never be among them. The one person he couldn't have.

Maybe he deserved the treat. Still, nothing on display sparked his desire.

Not when he'd recently been hip-to-hip with Sahara. Echoes of her scent and heat lingered on his skin.

How could he indulge his body in empty releases when the woman who owned his heart lived in the same city, even if she was out of reach?

Everyone stared at him as if expecting him to pick one or even more of the girls.

He hadn't seen so much female flesh on display since...

A memory flashed in his mind. The scared faces. The taunting voices. "Wetin be your own? Abi, you no de fuck woman?"

His stomach heaved, and a bitter tang filled his mouth.

"I'm sorry. I can't." He swivelled and walked out to the car park.

Shaking his head, he pushed the disgust and memories down.

"Hey, man. Are you okay?" Okey's shoes crunched on the sand and stone as he approached.

"I'm fine," he said in a snappy tone, then sucked in a calming breath. "I'm just tired."

Kane lifted his head and met the man's gaze, expecting to see disapproval. His old team had alienated him when he didn't join in their wicked depravity. There was no reason he should expect any difference from his former prison mate.

"Hey, man. I understand." Okey's acceptance stunned him.

"You don't mind? I thought you'd be angry after you'd gone to the effort of setting that up." He waved at the brothel.

"Of course, I'm not angry. I was in prison too, remember? I know what goes on in there. So I get it." He tapped his nose. "But if there is a specific type you like, then I can get Nnamdi to arrange to send one over to you."

It took Kane a few seconds to understand Okey's meaning. The man thought he preferred men.

He chuckled, opened his mouth to refute and shut it.

Perhaps Okey should think that he was gay rather than find out Kane was mad about his cousin. If Okey found out about Kane's past, especially his involvement with Sahara, Kane would be dead.

"There's no need. Good sleep will be enough for me," he said instead.

"Then, my friend, have a good night." Okey hugged him. "Nnamdi will be here at nine to pick you for the business we discussed."

"No problem. Goodnight," Kane said. "And thanks again."

Okey waved him off and got into the vehicle.

Kane checked in and asked the guy at reception to send someone to buy him some toiletries. In his room, he undressed and showered. Afterwards, he settled on the soft mattress, between fresh sheets and dreamt about the beautiful woman with the bow-shaped lips and luscious curves.

The next morning Kane was up before dawn, a habit of a lifetime. It took him seconds to realise he wasn't in the cramped cell or the hard plank bed.

He was out of jail, something he didn't think would happen soon.

He'd seen Sahara again. Another event he'd classed as highly unlikely.

All in one day.

Never believing in second chances, he'd given up on his life and had accepted to drift and suffer as punishment for the things he'd done.

Fate had offered him the opportunity to re-do his life and fix his mistakes.

Seeing Sahara again couldn't be just a coincidence. It had to mean something.

She was angry at him. She had every right to be mad at him, at the man he had been when they'd met.

He wasn't that person anymore.

Today was a crunch day.

If he would stay in the city, first he had to prove to Okey that he could deliver on his promise to sort out the man in the customs office. He had to make himself indispensable.

Then he would prove to Sahara that he was trustworthy and reliable. That he would always do the right thing by her.

Mind made up, he got out of bed and went into the shower. Afterwards, he stared at the jeans and shirt he'd worn the previous day. He needed new clothes. Would there be time to buy a new outfit before Nnamdi arrived?

Tapping on the door drew his attention.

He strode over and opened it. "Yes?"

A tall skinny light-skinned lad carried a package in his hands. "My name is Binyerem. Madam Rosa said I should give this to you."

It probably contained the toiletries he'd ordered last night.

He waved the boy in. "Put it on the table."

Binyerem sauntered into the room and put the small box on the desk. His lashes fluttered as he lowered his gaze. "Is there anything else I can help you with?"

The smart black tunic the lad wore got Kane's attention. "Do you know where I can get shirts like yours?"

The lad grinned. "Sure. My mother is a tailor, and I'm a fashion student although we're on school break at the moment. I can bring you a selection of the ready-made items, and you can pick what you want."

"Great." He didn't have a lot of cash. Hopefully, the clothes wouldn't be expensive. "I need two shirts and trousers."

He could wear his jeans most days, but he noticed that Okenna and Nnamdi were smartly dressed and he needed to blend in with them if he was hanging around for a few more days.

Binyerem pulled out a small digital device from his pocket and waved it over Kane.

"Okay. I'll be back in about thirty minutes."

"Wait a minute. How do you know my size?"

The boy gave him a coy smile again and raised the device in this hand. "Don't worry, sir. I know your size."

The device must have scanned his measurements.

Kane nodded. "I'll see you in thirty minutes."

"Okay, sir." The door slammed as Binyerem rushed out.

Kane opened the box and took out the toiletries he needed. Then he went in the bathroom, trimmed the beard down and shaved the moustache, leaving the hair short around his jaw line.

He stared at his reflection in the mirror. He wasn't clean-shaven. However, he no longer looked like a ruffian. With his hair combed out and in the correct clothes, he could pass for a businessman.

He just had to prove that he was a man worthy of this existence, of this life he'd landed in. A man deserving of the woman he loved.

Kiru Taye

CHAPTER FIVE

Binyerem returned in less than the quoted time with a small suitcase. He fussed over Kane like a mother hen, showing him clothes that matched his skin-tone and eye colour.

Kane had never cared about such things. Clothes were about function rather than aesthetics. He bought outfits because he needed them. Not as fashion statements.

But Binyerem talked about fabrics and textures and colours and styles.

In the end, Kane didn't argue with the lad's suggestions. He bought two button-up shirts and two tunics as well as a pair of formal black trousers.

His budget was blown, and he would need a job sooner rather than later.

Hopefully, the task he planned to undertake for Okey today would be a sort of job interview and land him a regular gig.

He was dressed in a blue tunic, black trousers and polished boots when Nnamdi arrived at his door. They walked down to the car where Okenna sat in the back seat.

"Morning," Kane said as he joined him.

Okey grinned. "You look like you slept well."

"I did. Thank you."

Nnamdi drove the car, joining the flow of commuter traffic.

"Good. We're heading to the wharf to see the man I told you about." Okenna pulled out a digital device from his jacket pocket and handed it to Kane. "This is the information we have on him."

On the screen, the file name was marked Suleiman above a picture of a middle-aged man who stood outside a warehouse dressed in the grey uniform of the Customs Service. There were other photos of the same man in civvies—long tunics, trousers and hula caps—at different locations including one with a woman and two male children in front of what looked like a family home. The annotations included his home address, work address, contact details, names of relatives, mistresses and known associates.

Kane read the details, storing vital facts in his memory.

Seeing the data on Mr Suleiman didn't shock him. In his previous life working for the government, they had kept dossiers on individuals they considered persons of interest and had used the insights for maximum impact in achieving their aims.

In any case, he needed as much personal info about the man so he could 'persuade' him easily. Although he'd been out of action for years, his mind slipped into mission mode with ease, his body primed for action.

At the wharf, they were cleared through the security checkpoint, and Nnamdi pulled into a spot in the parking lot.

"We'll wait for you here. Good luck," Okey said, remaining in his seat.

"Thanks," Kane muttered as he got out and strode into the sizeable two-level building.

A buzz of excitement went through him. He had missed the rush of having a mission and being on active duty. He'd missed having a purpose to his life.

He counted the number of guards on patrol as well as the closed-circuit cameras. He went through the full-body scanner before approaching the man at the lobby counter. "I'm here to see Mr Suleiman."

"And your name is?" the receptionist asked.

"Mr Waziri," he replied.

The man pressed a button on the desk console, spoke into his headset before handing Kane a visitor's pass. "Go up the stairs, turn left into the corridor. Mr Suleiman is in the last office on your right."

He already knew where the target was located from the dossier as well as the floor plan in case he needed an alternative exit.

He sucked in a deep breath and blew it out slowly to quell the surge of adrenaline in his veins.

Usually, on other missions, he had backup or operated as part of a team. However, prison had educated him on how to survive as a lone wolf.

There would be no fallback if he got into difficulty. Okey and Nnamdi would not come to his rescue. They wouldn't offer him a job if he didn't pass this test. Failure wasn't an option.

He found the office with a plaque saying 'Deputy Assistant Comptroller General' above Mr Suleiman's name.

Exhaling another deep breath, he knocked on the door.

"*Shigo*," a male voice invited him inside in Hausa.

He twisted the handle and pushed.

Mr Suleiman sat behind a desk with a monitor and keyboard, dressed in the grey uniform without the green beret. There were framed photographs of the president and the head of the Customs Service on the wall along with the coat of arms.

"*Sannu*," Kane greeted. "I'm Mr Waziri."

"Ah, Mr Waziri, *barka da zuwa*." The man stood and welcomed him with a smile, waving at the low padded seats around a coffee table. "Make yourself comfortable."

"*Na gode. Da fatan kuna lafiya?*" he replied with more pleasantries for the sake of keeping the man sweet. Hopefully, he could wrap this up in the same vein.

"*Ina lafiya godiya.* Can I get you some tea?" Mr Suleiman lifted the handset on the table and buzzed the intercom instructing the person on the other end to bring refreshments.

Kane allowed him to go through the rituals of entertaining a guest. After all, he was playing at being a businessman, and this was part of the negotiations.

A few minutes later, a uniformed woman in a grey skirt and white shirt brought a tray with a white teapot and cup set. She greeted the men and poured the drinks before leaving. She didn't make eye contact with either man which Kane found strange.

Until Kane noticed the way Mr Suleiman's leering gaze lingered on the woman's behind as she walked away. Was there something going on between the two of them? The woman had appeared uncomfortable and had done her job quickly and departed.

"Thank you for seeing me at such short notice," he said in a bid to dispel his discomfort at what he'd witnessed.

"Of course." The man took a sip from the cup. "I don't see many of my people in this part of the country. So whenever I see a name I recognise, I make sure the person is given top priority."

Kane's heart skipped a beat. "You recognise my name?"

"Of course. You're my brother, one of us. I know a Waziri family from Sokoto. Brigadier General Sani Waziri at the State Security Services. Are you related to him?"

Shit. The man didn't know how close to home he had hit.

He schooled his expression and nodded. "I know the family."

It wasn't a lie. But not the whole truth either.

"Good." Mr Suleiman relaxed into his heat. "We were in the military academy together, although we took different paths."

The man acquired a faraway look as if he was reminiscing about the old days.

"About my reason for being here," Kane said, wanting to avoid being drawn into a discussion about family. "I was hoping we could come to some arrangement about the Odili Imports."

"Odili Imports? What does that have to do with you?" Suleiman frowned.

"I was hired as a consultant to help negotiate a deal with you," Kane said.

"Ah. They hired you. Those arrogant men? They walk around as if they own this town. They come in here, in their flashy suits and expensive cars and expect us to do what they want. I will show them that we are the ones in charge."

The man's suddenly belligerent tone made Kane stiffen.

Was the he just being diligent? Or was there something more sinister going on?

"I understand your anger. But this is business, and they will pay you a reasonable price to reach a deal with you."

"No." Suleiman sipped his tea.

Maybe the fellow was principled and didn't accept bribes. Yet, the dossier had included amounts of monies given to Suleiman by other importers. Was that incorrect?

"Is there nothing that can persuade you to work with Odili Imports?" Kane had to find something which would appeal to him. "Nothing at all?"

"No. That nonsense infidel, Okenna, or whatever his name is, dared to touch my niece. That's why he was sent to prison."

"Oh. Did he assault your niece?" Kane's hackles rose.

Okey hadn't told Kane why he was in prison. Had he done something to Suleiman's relative?

"He might as well have done. He had no rights to touch her with his filthy hands," the man griped.

Kane still wasn't clear on the situation. This could be a game-changer. He would gun for his ex jail mate, if the allegation proved correct. He had zero tolerance for sexual assault perpetrators.

"Sir, I need to understand what you're saying. Did Okenna assault your niece?" Kane used the tone he reserved for people under interrogation.

The man tugged his collar and shifted in his seat. "No."

"So why would Okenna be sent to prison if he did nothing wrong?"

"I wanted him to be punished for corrupting my niece. She had been a good girl at university until she became involved with him."

"Ah, I see." This was about the man's prejudice rather than any wrongdoing by Okey.

"Look, I'll tell you something." Suleiman leaned forward and lowered his voice. "I don't like these Igbo people at all. And you see that Odili family, I hate them even more. And I will do anything to frustrate their businesses."

Revulsion filled Kane's mouth with a bitter tang at the man's blatant tribalistic prejudice. He'd witnessed similar retrogressive xenophobic attitudes before and knew this represented everything terrible in this country.

He'd been obligated to protect those sons of bitches while he'd been in the military service.

No more.

"If you dislike these people so much, why do you choose to work in their state?" Kane tried to keep his distaste out of his voice.

Suleiman's shoulders rose and fell. "Because the state is part of the country and we run this country. We are untouchable. I can go anywhere I want. Do whatever I want." The man spoke with a feverish zeal and then his lips twisted in a leer. "And let me tell you one good reason to live here. Their women are easy. So promiscuous."

Kane narrowed his eyes. The man's misogyny got on his nerves. "No more than women from other tribes."

Suleiman's laughter echoed in the large office. "Are you married?"

"No," Kane replied curtly.

"Good. The only reason you defend these *baki* is because you're fucking one of them. Yes, they are sweet but not suitable wife material for us."

Kane's gripped the arms of the chair tight, fighting to control his rising anger. "That's not a nice thing to say about a woman."

The man was vile and crazy, and he was in a position of power, for goodness sake.

"She really must be sweet." Suleiman licked his fat lips. "I will reconsider my stance about the Odili Imports if I get to fuck her too. Bring—"

He didn't finish whatever disgusting thing he was about to say because Kane shot off the chair, grabbed the teapot and smashed it into his skull.

The idea of the man touching Sahara in any way stripped him of the cloak of normalcy he'd worn since his release from prison. The remorseless killer he'd tried to bury rose to the fore to protect.

His heart rate spiked and adrenaline rushed through his veins. His mind switched from mediation to combat mode.

Stunned, Suleiman cried out and clutched his head. Crimson and amber liquid spilled down his face as cracked ceramic chips scattered on the floor.

Kane yanked his head back, picked a jagged piece and stuck it at the man's throat deep enough to nick the skin. A small movement could cause irreparable damage.

Suleiman froze in place.

"People like you disgust me," Kane gritted out in a hard voice. "You are the reason this country is rotten. Enough is enough." He dug the sharp tip close to Suleiman's jugular vein. "I am your worst nightmare. I could gut you right here like the pig that you are and walk out of the door. No one will stop me."

"You can't do that," the man mumbled. "I'll call security."

"Oh, I can. Have you ever heard about the Death Squad? You're looking at the Grim Reaper himself. We make people disappear every day. I can make you disappear. I know members of your family and where you live. I can pay your wife a visit."

"No!" The man trembled, his eyes wide with terror.

The Death Squad was widely regarded as a myth, and the name given to a notorious covert military team set up by the DSS to carry out reconnaissance and assassinations. Of course the government had never admitted to having such a group and always dismissed the claims as conspiracy theories.

However, Kane was living proof that the team existed. He wasn't altogether proud of all the things he'd done in the name of his country.

A knot tightened in his stomach when he thought about the woman he had lost because of his job.

"You don't like your wife being threatened, do you?" Kane's voice was cold and deadly, his anger rising again. "And yet you had the effrontery to insult mine."

Another half-truth.

Sahara had once agreed to be his wife.

Then he'd screwed up.

Even if she never agreed to be his wife again, it didn't give the man the rights to denigrate her.

"I'm sorry," Suleiman begged. "I didn't know she was your wife."

"She is mine, under my protection. Just like the Odilis are now under my protection. So if you want to live, sign the authorisation to allow their containers to clear customs now."

"Yes. Yes, I'll do it." The man bobbed his head.

"Get up."

The man complied and stumbled to the desk. Kane kept pace with him to make sure he didn't raise the alarm.

Suleiman slumped into his chair and fumbled on the keyboard with one hand. The screen saver unlocked, and he logged into the Custom Service servers. A few more clicks and electronic certification was completed.

"I want a paper copy," Kane said.

Suleiman's hand trembled as he pressed a button. The printer on the desk buzzed and a paper slid out.

Kane grabbed it. "You know better than to get the police involved. Trust me. If I have to come back for you, a gash in the head will be the least of your problems."

"Yes ... I—I understand."

"Good. You now work for me. Anytime I need anything sorted out in Customs you will be my man. Understood?"

"Y—yes."

"Clean yourself up. You look a mess."

Kane tossed the broken piece onto the floor and walked out of the man's office.

Hopefully, the fear of his threat would keep Suleiman compliant. It had been effective with others before. It should work this time.

Otherwise, Kane had just earned himself a one-way ticket back to jail.

CHAPTER SIX

Sahara exited the library building and halted. Her heart slammed against her ribcage.

The setting sun hung low on the horizon behind the trees, casting long shadows.

A man leaned against the metal fence separating the parking lot from the glass and steel building of the learning centre. He pulled out a vape stick from his shirt pocket and raised the eCig to his mouth, taking a slow, steady, gentle inhale. Vapour swirled around him in white mist.

Kane.

It had been two weeks since she'd seen him. Two weeks since she'd walked into Olivia Restaurant and found him having a meal with Okenna.

When her cousin had told her that he knew a man who could sort out his problems with Customs, she hadn't known the man in question would be the same man she'd loved, the man who had turned into a nightmare.

Years ago as an undergrad she'd met Kane who had been a post-grad, or so she'd thought. They had dated for almost a year and had made plans for the future.

Then she'd found out the truth about him.

He hadn't been studying, after all. But an undercover agent sent to infiltrate an anti-government student group. She'd been a member of the same organisation.

Needless to say, she'd been heartbroken when she'd found out the truth about him. After the disaster that had ensued, she'd had to change universities.

She hadn't seen him for half a decade until two weeks ago.

Why was he here?

She couldn't accept that by some random fate he'd turned up in her city and was now working for her father.

Then again, her father had been angry with her cousin since the debacle with Mr Suleiman's niece and Kane had saved Okey's neck by sorting out the problem.

Could this be a ruse for Kane to get into the Odili operations? Was he spying for the government?

There was only one way to find out.

She walked down the ramp towards the car park.

Her SUV stood in a spot. She had requested for Okey to send Kane to pick her up, making an excuse about her usual chauffeur being on an errand.

She wanted a chance to talk to Kane without interference from the rest of her family.

Too many eyebrows would rise if they suspected she had history with Kane. And she couldn't afford anyone shooting first and asking questions later.

Considering what Kane had done for Okey, she would give him the benefit of the doubt.

As she approached, Kane didn't look in her direction.

He'd filled out a little since she'd last seen him when he'd appeared gaunt and scraggly like a stray dog.

Now his hair had been cut down, looking less 'unkempt bush' and more 'mown lawn'. He even sported a designer beard. She could see the Binyerem influence in his clothes— black embroidered tunic, black trousers and polished shoes.

His skin looked healthier, and the pure athletic muscular body made her heart race and her skin warm.

Damn, he looked good. Better than good.

He wasn't handsome in a conventional way—his skin was a dark hickory shade, his cheekbones too sharp and his dark eyes had a glint of danger.

Once upon a time, he'd been charming and attentive. When he walked into a room, his presence commanded attention. He'd been hers though. None of the other girls had ever had a chance with him.

It seemed things hadn't changed in that regard.

He hadn't had sex with anyone since his arrival. Okey had offered him women from a brothel, and he'd turned them down. He hadn't been with anyone else.

She'd learnt a few things from him. Like how to spy on a suspect.

Until she figured out his reasons for being here, he would be treated as a suspect.

She'd sent Binyerem to Kane to gather info about what her ex did and with whom. When he wasn't working, he was at his apartment. Between information from Binyerem and Okey, she knew everyone he'd interacted with since he arrived.

Kane was a dangerous man and the lives of her family members were at stake, not to mention their businesses.

"Those things are going to kill you," she said in a sultry voice.

Kane glanced up as he switched off the vape stick. His breath hitched as he raised his hand to block the glare from the sun descending behind her.

He stared at her without guise or shame—with adoration, body posture open and expression soft.

Warmth spread across her chest.

Kane still found her attractive.

She wore a three-quarter length, loose-sleeved, mixed-print, cerulean dress which skimmed her curves and swirled around her ankles and stilettos. Her afro hair had been straightened with flat hot irons and draped on her shoulders, framing her face.

He'd once told her the colour of her hair reminded him of violet midnight and complemented the copper-penny shade of her skin now shown off by the v-shaped décolletage revealing her neck and chest.

His gaze lingered on the swells of her breasts, leaving a trail of heat as he admired her.

She loved that he didn't look away or watch her surreptitiously like some men did.

His heated gaze alone turned her on in ways no one else could.

Her heart beat rapidly, and her hands became clammy.

Damn it. She was going to need her battery-operated boyfriend by the time the night was over.

Kane was her ex, a traitor to her heart. She needed to get a grip.

She sucked in a shallow breath. "You know what. I take that back. I think my father will have you killed first when he sees the way you're staring at me."

The corner of his lips tugged up and he lifted his shoulders in a shrug. "There are fates worse than death."

His blasé tone gave ammunition to her suspicions.

"Yeah, you would say that, wouldn't you? So all the people you butchered in the service of your country—" she did air quotes with her fingers "—were mercy killings?"

His eyes narrowed, and his hands curled into fists. "You are hardly one to point fingers, daughter of the head of a cartel and all. Has your father never had anyone tortured or killed?"

How dare he?

Propelled by anger, she stepped into his personal space before she could think better of it. "My father has never slaughtered innocent civilians."

"Really? You know your father that well." He stared at her with dark, piercing, unflinching eyes.

Had to be a technique he learned in the military—how to stare down an opponent.

Her pulse accelerated and she struggled not to lower her gaze. Struggled with not taking the step needed to breach the gap between them and surrender her mouth and body to him.

"Yes, which is more than I can say for you." She glared at him, swivelled and walked towards the entrance to the park.

Safer to keep away from him before she did something she'd regret.

"Where are you going? The car is over there." He pointed in the opposite direction.

"I need some fresh air," she taunted with his words from two weeks ago and continued walking, knowing he would have to follow her.

Even if she didn't know anything else about him, Kane was protective. He'd gone out of his way to keep her safe before and had done so again recently with her cousin.

A park ranger approached her. "Madam, the park will close in ten minutes."

"I know. Just give us a little time." She raised her digital device from her shoulder bag.

He understood her meaning and pulled his out.

She clicked on the mobile money app and tapped his gadget with hers, transferring money into his personal account.

The man stared at his phone and grinned. "Thank you."

"You're welcome."

Sahara walked to a bench and sat down. Ducks and geese frolicked around the large pond. The place was almost deserted. The last people were packing up and leaving.

"What was that about?" Kane stopped beside the bench and pointed at the exit.

"I gave the park ranger a tip to allow me in here for a little longer." She rolled her head to the side to look at him.

He nodded but didn't sit down.

She didn't say anything for several minutes as they watched the sun disappear into the horizon. The sky went from orange to purple, and the shadows deepened. Calmness settled around them.

"I like to sit here and watch the sun go down," she said, melancholy seeping into her words. "It's beautiful."

"It is." Something in his voice made her turn in his direction.

He had that soft expression again. Was he referring to her as beautiful?

If only she could trust him, she would accept the things his eyes were saying and allow him to spread on the grass and make love to her.

She swallowed and averted her gaze. "The sunset reminds me of how precarious life can be—good one moment and bad the next—and tells me to savour the wonderful moments."

She'd once thought they had a beautiful life together until she found out their relationship had been based on lies.

She puffed out a heavy breath. There was no point dwelling on the past. She had to deal with the present. "Why are you still in the city, Kane? I told you to leave."

He lowered his body onto the opposite end of the bench and spoke in a matter-of-fact tone. "Okey offered me a job. I took it."

She straightened. The only lighting came from street lamps close to the perimeter fence. This bench sat in a dark corner, making it difficult to read his expression.

"I know he offered you a job? What I don't know is why you chose to stay when you have a job. Are you undercover?"

He puffed out a breath and scrubbed his face. "I'm not undercover."

"I don't believe you. Have you forgotten I know who you are and what you do for a living?"

He wouldn't admit it to her, would he, especially if her family was the target?

What if he was investigating her father? Worse, what if he was here to kill her dad?

A cold shiver went down her spine. She couldn't lose another parent, the way she'd lost her mother and brother.

"I'm not a DSS agent anymore. I was discharged years ago."

It took a few seconds for his words to register. Her mouth dropped open.

"Discharged?" She shook her head in disbelief and gaped at him. "How? The military is your life."

He had said those words to her many years ago.

"The military was my life. I want a different life now."

"Kane, I don't understand. What are you talking about?"

He puffed out another heavy breath. "After we broke up, things went bad. I became dissatisfied with my life and my job. I started questioning everything. Not a good idea when you're in the military. We are supposed to obey orders and not question them. My superiors were not happy. In the end, I was court-martialled for insubordination and conduct unbecoming of an officer."

"Wow." She slumped onto the bench and just stared at him for a few minutes. She still couldn't comprehend everything he'd said.

He'd been a first-class officer and captain of his unit. He had dedicated his life to the service, even going as far as seducing her all so he could get the job done.

"Is that why you were in prison?" she asked, thinking he would have been incarcerated when he was court-martialled.

"No. I would have been sent to the military penal camp. My life spiralled out of control after I became a civilian. I guess it was a mixture of not having a regimented life and missing you."

Her heart skipped a beat. Had she heard correctly? "Missing me?"

His Adam's apple bobbed. "My life wasn't the same after you. I haven't been the same—"

There were *whoosh whoosh* sounds of rushing blood in her ears.

"Enough! I won't listen to your lies. I won't fall for them again." Her throat clogged up.

She'd loved him, damn it. And he'd lied to her, and used her for his investigations.

Not again.

Standing, she pulled the 9mm Beretta Nano from her purse and pointed it at his chest.

His eyes widened, but he didn't get up. "Sahara—"

"No. You listen."

"Okay." He relaxed into his seat as if he wasn't afraid.

She tightened her grip on the gun, keeping it level with his head.

"Five years ago, you came into my life, made me fall in love with you and promised me a future together.

Meanwhile you lied to me and I was simply a means to an end for your mission. You arrested my fellow students, some who were my friends. I don't even want to think about the torture some of them went through while in captivity."

She clutched her bag to her midriff to hide her body's trembling.

"I picked up the pieces of my life and moved on. Then you show up and all I felt the night I saw you at Olivia's was rage. How dare you just waltz into my life as if nothing's happened? Then Okey told me how you helped him out and I thought, maybe I could give you a break. Maybe I could have a chat with you and get closure."

She swallowed the lump in her throat. "But I swear to God, if you tell me one more lie, I will shoot right here."

"I swear to you," Kane said and he got off the bench, hands raised in a placating manner. "I haven't told you a lie this evening or since I arrived here."

"Stay back," she warned when he moved in her direction.

"I'm not a threat to you." He kept walking towards her until his chest became flushed with the nozzle of the gun. He didn't grab the weapon. "I would rather die than give you false information again."

How could he not be a threat? She'd seen him in ruthless action before. He'd duped her.

She should shoot him right now and end the trouble to come from him.

Her finger above the trigger trembled. Her chest tightened, making it difficult to breath.

She couldn't hurt him, damn it.

Was he telling the truth?

"How am I supposed to trust you?"

"Pull the trigger and end my life right now. That's the power you have over me. You hold my heart, my life, in your hands," he said in a quiet voice as if he'd accepted his fate.

"Don't say that." Her voice shook. She stepped back, lowering the gun.

"I mean it. I regret not telling you I was an undercover DSS agent on time."

He stepped closer, demolishing the gap between them. His voice grew husky. "I fell apart without you. The job became a grind. I love you, Sa. Please give me another chance to prove it to you."

He sounded sincere and she wanted to believe him. Everyone who was repentant deserved a second chance, especially when it seemed he'd been punished and had suffered as a result of his action.

"Promise me no more lies."

"On my life."

"Okay."

Puffing out a breath, he lowered his hands and grabbed the gun, clicked the safety back in place and lowered it onto the bench.

Then he scooped her into his arms and kissed her.

CHAPTER SEVEN

Finally she was in his arms. The woman Kane loved was giving him a second chance.

To think he'd given up on ever seeing her again, let alone getting together with her.

No more screw ups. She was his 'ride or die'.

Sahara's hands slid up his chest. Her palms burnt his skin through the fabric of his shirt.

He wanted her hands and lips all over. He physically ached, throbbed for her.

Wanting more of her, he tilted his head and deepened the kiss. It had been ages since he'd tasted her and she was the best cocktail—sweet and intoxicating—making him lose control.

He ravaged her mouth and grabbed her ass, grinding their hips together.

She moaned, her fingers clutching his shoulders as she returned his kiss with passion.

"Oh, I missed you so much," he whispered against her mouth before trailing his lips across her cheek to her ear lobe.

"I missed you too," she said in a breathy voice.

He guided her onto the bench and resealed their lips.

She ground her hips against his bulge, eliciting a strangled moan from him.

He swelled painfully. He'd been hard as a rock from the moment he'd seen her standing in the car park as stunning as ever.

She canted her body and he groaned again.

"You're going to be the death of me," he said between panting breaths. In more ways than one, she could lead to his demise.

First of all, they were in a public park at night. Secondly, she was his boss's daughter and out of bounds to him.

He should stop, and end this thing before it ended him.

From the moment he kissed her, he went beyond the point of caring.

If his life was the price he paid to have these stolen moments with her, he'd accept it.

"If you don't get on with it, then let me go home and get BOB to do the job for you," she said in a teasing voice.

"Who the hell is Bob?" He gripped her face as his chest burned with jealousy that she could have a lover at home.

She giggled, the sound musical. "BOB, my battery-operated boyfriend."

"Hell, no." Relief washed over him and he grinned. "From now on, you're not allowed any sex toys without my permissions.

"Whatever you say, Captain." She fluttered her lashes as she laughed some more.

His heart skipped several beats.

Damn. She'd used 'captain' as a term of endearment when they'd first met and he'd told her of his military designation.

Now the word fuelled his hunger for her. The idea of stopping vanished into the night.

He pulled down the front of her dress, exposing dark nipples as he bit into the left fleshy mound.

"Oh," she cried out, body arching.

Yes! He'd missed the pleasure-driven noises she made.

Bringing his right hand around, he pulled up her dress until he could reach her panties unimpeded. He dug his index finger into the lace and tore it. Then he found what he was looking for; silky wetness made his digits slide over her pussy.

Another moan escaped from her.

"Keep your voice down or the park ranger is going to investigate." His voice sounded hoarse and raw as he fought for some restraint.

This was Sahara, his Sahara. He'd never wanted anyone more than he wanted her. And he was going to make her come apart on a bench in the middle of the park at night.

Her lashes fluttered against her cheeks and she moved restlessly. "I need you, Kane."

"What do you need?" He teased her labia with his fingers.

"Your hand, your mouth. You." Her response erased his restraint.

"Do you want me to eat your pussy?"

"Yes, please!" Her eyes blazed with fire, and her body trembled beneath his touch.

He slid down and pulled the rest of her tattered panty off. Then he spread her thighs, opening her up to his gaze, her dress scrunched around her waist in a shimmer of silk. Below, she glimmered, brown and beautiful, her clit swollen and erect, framed by trimmed wisps of brown hair. She smelled of musk and Sahara.

Considering their location, she displayed both vulnerability and strength, exposed to his gaze and not covering her body. Her complete surrender humbled him, made him want to be the best man he could be. He would protect her and possess her with all that he was and all he could ever be.

He closed his eyes and sucked in a long breath. Her image burned his mind. Her sweet scent filled his lungs. Her skin felt soft and satiny under his palm. His body thrummed, hummed with his craving for her. Seeing her again, he'd known he couldn't walk away.

"Tell me there's no one else. Tell me you're mine, Sa, and I will give you what you need.

She stared at him with lust-filled heavy-lidded eyes. "I'm yours, Kane."

Her words were a balm to his soul and fire in his veins. He had to taste her.

Lowering his head, he swiped his tongue from her slit to her clit. She nearly shot off the bench. He clamped a hand across her belly, holding her down.

"My sweet Sa." He licked his lips, savouring her feminine tang before licking her again. "Do you want more?"

She keened and arched her body, pushing her hips toward his mouth.

"Mmhm." She nodded. Sweat glistened on her forehead, and her long dark lashes fanned her cheeks as she lowered her eyelids. The tip of her pink tongue darted out and licked her lower lip.

He started off with light teases, licking and swiping his tongue around the lower lips, before trailing down to her slit and tunnelling in with the tip. It had been so long since he'd worshiped her body in this manner. He would make time to give her all the kinds of pleasure she enjoyed.

Using his left hand to part her labia, he took her clit into his mouth and sucked gently. She moaned, writhed, her body winding tight. He used his right index finger to swipe her juices and slid it down the crease of her ass. He pressed it against her pucker, and she groaned when he worked in and she clamped around him. Her body wound tight, her moans getting louder and louder, he knew she wasn't far from her climax.

"Kane. I'm..."

"It's okay, Sa. I've got you."

He sucked harder on her clit, and she detonated under him. Her body thrashed for seconds on end as she let out a long scream of his name that echoed in his head again and again. He slid up and pulled her into his arms before taking her mouth in an intense kiss. She clung to him, returning his kiss with as much passion as he did.

Afterwards, he pocketed her pants and tidied up her dress.

She snuggled next to him on the bench and he wrapped his arms around her. They sat quietly for a few minutes as he fought to get his body under control. He would take himself in hand when he got to his apartment as he replayed the image of her on the park bench.

"Kane," she trailed her finger down his chest towards his groin. "Won't you finish what we started?"

He held her hand still. "Baby, I don't want the park ranger to interrupt us when I'm inside you. I don't want him to see you. You're for my eyes only."

She sighed and burrowed deeper. "When am I going to see you again after tonight? You can't exactly show up at my father's house. At least not yet. Not until you prove yourself among the Yadili."

He brushed his knuckles down her cheek. "I'll figure out a way for us to be together regularly. I promise."

"I know. Worse case, we'll meet in the park. We could even camp out here all night." Her eyes glimmered in the dark.

"And give the park ranger a huge tip." He kissed her briefly. "Come on. Let me take you home."

They walked out hand-in-hand. In the car, Sahara sat up front with him.

"Tell me why you went to jail," she asked when they got on the road.

He glanced at her before returning his gaze to the road.

He didn't like talking about that shitty part of his life. Still, he'd promised not to keep any secrets from her.

"I went to jail because I got into a drunken brawl and beat a guy to a pulp..." he kept it brief. She didn't need the details. After a few heartbeats, he added, "Then I met Okey, and I found out he was related to you."

Meeting her cousin in jail had been a miracle. No other way to describe it since it had led him right to this point.

"He told me you saved his life in prison," she said while caressing his right arm, through the tunic sleeve.

Probably one of the best things he'd done in his life.

"I couldn't let them hurt him. I knew how disappointed you'd been when your student friends were arrested. You blamed me. I imagined how mad you would be if you found out he was in jail with me and got injured."

"So you helped him because of me?" She beamed a smile, making his chest tingle.

"Yes, and I thought the fight was unfair anyway. There were five of them against just one of him."

"Thank you for what you did for him in prison and for sorting out his problem with Customs. Now, my father has forgiven him."

"Your father? Why?"

She puffed out a heavy breath. "The problem started when Okey was dating Adia Suleiman."

"That's the customs officer's niece?"

"Yes. Okenna was in love with the girl. He wanted to marry her. But when her family found out, they didn't want him near her and accused him of rape."

"I heard about that. How come your father didn't prevent him from going to jail?"

Her hand on his arm stilled and she glanced at him.

"You have to understand one thing about this life. Family is everything. And when I say family, I don't just mean Odili. I mean Yadili. Every member of the Yadili network is a part of the family. They swear an oath of allegiance to my father, and he adopts them as his sons. Yadili is founded on trust, loyalty and honour. So my father treats everybody equally?"

"So he couldn't give special treatment to his nephew?" Kane asked. In a country where nepotism had become rampant, it was refreshing to see someone play by different rules.

"Exactly. Okenna's affair messed up the business when customs banned Odili Imports. That's a major problem, and the business was losing millions with the restrictions. My father said that if he was foolish enough to get involved with somebody he shouldn't have then he should be ready to pay the consequences."

"Going to jail?"

"Yes. Dad thought the guys at customs would relax the ban if Okey pleaded guilty to assault and went to jail. But the ban continued even after he'd served his term, which was why he needed your help with Mr Suleiman."

"I'm glad I could help. Mr Suleiman is a nasty piece of work." Kane remembered the vile man.

"I was worried Okey would be expelled from Yadili. Now he is back in my father's good graces. All thanks to you."

"You don't have to thank me."

She nodded. "So what about you? Do you really want to stay here and work for Okenna? The men see you as an outsider."

"I don't mind." He shrugged. He couldn't think of a life without her in it. "I want to be wherever you are. And from what you said, I could become Yadili."

She giggled. "You, Yadili? You're not Igbo."

He stiffened. "Is there a rule that says only Igbos can be Yadilis?"

"No. I don't think so."

"Or does your father have a problem against Hausa men?"

It was her turn to stiffen. "Of course not."

"So there's no reason I can't become one."

Even if his chance was one percent he would still take it. Sahara was everything and getting the chance to belong again to a band of brothers was a bonus.

"I guess so," she said with a smile that lit up her face. "You will have to prove yourself worthy of the oath."

"I will do whatever it takes." He lifted her hand and pressed a kiss to her knuckles.

"Okay." She paused and tilted her head towards him. "Hang on a minute. Why do you want to become Yadili?"

He glanced at her again and spoke honestly. "I realise that it's probably the only way your family will trust me enough to let me marry you."

Her breath hitched and she straightened. "You want to marry me? Are you proposing again?"

He pulled the car to a stop, turned to face her and took her soft hands in his. "I've wanted to marry you since the first day I met you. I have no future without you in it. I'm here to stay, if you will let me."

She bit her lower lip as her bright eyes caught the light.

"Yes, on one condition. You must earn your place as Yadili and swear allegiance to my father."

He leaned across and pressed his lips to hers. "You have a deal."

HONOUR is the prequel to the upcoming romantic suspense story THE RISE OF KANE which is out in 2020.

ABOUT THE AUTHOR

Kiru Taye is the award-winning author of sensual African stories. When she couldn't find stories of Africans falling in love, she decided to write the stories she wanted to read. She has written over twenty romance novels and lives in the UK with her family.

Connect with Kiru:
https://www.kirutaye.com/

Thank you for reading Love and the Lawless.
If you enjoyed the stories please leave a review.

OTHER BOOKS BY LOVE AFRICA PRESS

Diary of a Wallflower by Glory Abah

Unravelling His Mark by Zee Monodee

Healing His Medic by Nana Prah

Dawsk by Erhu Kome Yellow

Find out more:
www.loveafricapress.com